What began with a wink, ends in the clink.

"We have three suspects that we need to narrow down to one." I grabbed George's arm and looked at her watch. "We have four hours. Four hours and counting until the award ceremony."

"What do we do now?" said Bess.

"I suck it up and go get a fro-yo," I said, reluctantly. "Find Aly at the stand and get answers."

"Why don't we all go?" George suggested.

"Strength in numbers," said Bess.

"No, girls," I said. "I have to go this one alone. We'll have a better shot at getting the information if I'm by myself. It'll be okay. I just need to do my best to avoid Heather Harris."

"What if she's there?" asked Bess.

"Then I'll just have to deal as best I can."

NANCY DREW

GIRL DETECTIVE

Available from Aladdin

CAROLYN KEENE

NANCY DREW
GIRL DETECTIVE®

Sabotage Surrender

#44

**Book Three in the
Sabotage Mystery Trilogy**

Aladdin
New York   London   Toronto   Sydney

❧ ALADDIN
An imprint of Simon & Schuster Children's Publishing Division
1230 Avenue of the Americas, New York, NY 10020
First Aladdin paperback edition February 2011
Copyright © 2011 by Simon & Schuster
All rights reserved, including the right of reproduction in whole or in part in any form.
ALADDIN is a trademark of Simon & Schuster, Inc., and related logo is a registered trademark of Simon & Schuster, Inc.
NANCY DREW, NANCY DREW: GIRL DETECTIVE, and related logo are registered trademarks of Simon & Schuster, Inc.
For information about special discounts for bulk purchases, please contact Simon & Schuster Special Sales at 1-866-506-1949 or business@simonandschuster.com.
The Simon & Schuster Speakers Bureau can bring authors to your live event. For more information or to book an event contact the Simon & Schuster Speakers Bureau at 1-866-248-3049 or visit our website at www.simonspeakers.com.
Designed by Karina Granda
The text of this book was set in Bembo.
Manufactured in the United States of America
0111 OFF
10 9 8 7 6 5 4 3 2 1
Library of Congress Control Number 2010937262
ISBN 978-1-4169-9071-0
ISBN 978-1-4424-1954-4 (eBook)

2176

Table of Contents

DAY THREE

I clutched my oversize paper Club Coffee cup and swished the cold, sugary dregs of caffeine around. I took a sip and winced at what had once been a delicious drink.

Earlier this morning it had been an extra-large caramel macchiato with extra caramel drizzled over the extra whipped cream with an extra shot of espresso. Earlier this morning it had been amazing and warm and delicious. Sadly, now the coffee was cold and bitter and no longer a priority for me after an hour of sitting in the front office of the school, watching the video footage of the thief over and over.

My only hope was that Bess or George would remember to bring me another caramel macchiato when they arrived later. Fingers crossed! To make sure, I pulled out my PDA and sent them each a text as a reminder.

EXTRA-LARGE CARAMEL MACCHIATO.
EXTRA CARAMEL DRIZZLED OVER
EXTRA WHIPPED CREAM. ADD AN
EXTRA SHOT OF ESPRESSO.

Bess responded first. omg!

George responded next. lol!

As for the thief, I'd watched the video footage, endlessly, on repeat—but I still couldn't make out much about the actual thief. I had been poring over every inch of the screen. It was a somewhat shorter man dressed all in black, and that was about all I could see. Whoever he was he'd stolen the cash box full of carnival ticket money and gone to great lengths to make sure he couldn't be identified by covering his tracks, casting blame onto others who happened to be in the area, and concealing any of his identifiable features such as hair color. A real professional, if you asked me.

The creepiest detail of all was that he seemed to know where the cameras were stationed around the school and therefore strategically kept to the shadows and out of their line of sight. Once in possession of the cash box, the thief had left the ticket booth and then immediately disappeared. This knowledge of the cameras' location indicated a certain familiarity with the school. But how so? Was he a teacher? A current student? A former student? An administrator? A member of the janitorial staff? He had done an expert job, mapping out a near-perfect escape route, avoiding additional security cameras, and leaving little evidence behind. In fact, leaving behind only this footage.

So far in my review of the tape, all I'd noticed was that he'd stopped to scratch a spot to the bottom left of his collar a couple of times before placing his hands on the cash box to steal it away. This spot really seemed to bother him for some reason.

But by my seventeenth view or so of the footage, I noticed something different.

If you blinked, you would have missed it.

I watched it some more, and the more I watched the footage, the more clearly the gesture became somewhat of a clue to go on. The mystery man stopped, looked up toward the camera, and winked. He *actually* winked!

It was kind of far away and not the clearest of footage, granted, but I also knew a wink when I saw one. Yes, admittedly, I sometimes tended to take my cases a bit too personally, since I *was* the one who tended to solve them, rather than law enforcement, but for some reason I felt as though that wink was directed right at me. Like he knew I was hot on his trail. This only made me want to solve the mystery even more. I mean, how could it not have been directed at me? I had been on the trail of this criminal for two days now, moving into a third. I wanted nothing more than to bring this whole string of criminal activity to a close.

I hit rewind again and sat as close to the screen as I could without going cross-eyed. Mrs. Gruen— our housekeeper and a mother figure to me—would have yelled at me if she walked in and seen me. She loved to say that I would go blind if I sat too close to the television. I shrugged away her voice in my head, scolding me, and looked for the thief's wink again. There it was—*wink!* I couldn't tell you what color those eyes were, but one of them was definitely winking, as if to tell me he knew I was onto him. The wink was an acknowledgment that he was smarter than the police, smarter than me, and he wasn't going to get caught.

According to my PDA, the time was 7:42 a.m.—

eighteen minutes before the rest of the carnival volunteers would begin to show up and set up their stations.

"This could be considered breaking and entering, you know." A deep voice broke the silence I'd settled into ages ago, making me jump about a foot out of my seat. "I'd hate to see you get arrested."

I whipped around, half expecting the dark-hooded, ski-masked figure I'd been watching on the television monitor to be glaring back at me, maybe winking at me.

The playful, warm brown eyes and smiling, gorgeous face of my boyfriend, Ned Nickerson, appeared before me. "You scared me, Ned. I'm glad to see that it's you and not someone else. I thought for a second you were our mystery man."

Ned held out his hands. "Easy," he soothed. "I've been cleared of all charges, remember? I am not responsible. I'm not the thief."

Still distracted by the footage, I said, "I am looking at the thief right now."

His arms were crossed over his chest as he looked at me with a sweet yet accusing look. "I hope you haven't been here all night," he said. "Last time I left you, you were looking at this footage. Tell me you went home. Tell me you didn't sleep here."

"I didn't sleep here, Ned."

"How long have you been here?"

"Only an hour," I said, pointing to the video footage. I rose from my seat and wrapped my arms around Ned, squeezing him as tight as I could. "How could I forget?" I asked. "It's great to see you free and not behind bars."

Ned laughed. "You totally would have come and visited me in jail."

"Thankfully, I didn't let the situation get to that point."

Yesterday, Ned had been the first suspect in the theft of the cash box money. Just because he was working at the ticket booth and *maybe* . . . okay, *definitely* dozed off for a while, providing a moment for the thief to break into the booth and steal the cash box. So even though he didn't steal the money, he had a certain amount of blame in the whole thing.

Now don't get me wrong, I'm still mad at Ned for falling asleep at the counter. I mean, who *does* that? I'm just thankful that I was there to help prove his innocence. Otherwise, Mark Steele, the head of the carnival committee, and Chief McGinnis would have most likely arrested him.

People really had been treating this year's annual River Heights' Celebration differently. The reason? It seemed more important than years past—mostly,

I assumed, due to Mrs. Mahoney's involvement. Thanks to her generosity (and the money her late husband, Cornelius, left her in his will when he passed), everything was much more grand this year.

The rides, the food—even the traditional Daughter of River Heights Celebration parade were all more extravagant than ever.

Or at least, they were supposed to be.

Before the sabotage began.

Sabotage had become the word of the hour throughout this celebration. The rides, the cash box, even the food had been sabotaged, with a grill fire and food poisoning. Mara Stanfield, the president of the Daughters of River Heights Association, had a brick with a nasty note thrown through her house window. The cash from ticket sales wasn't just going back to Mrs. Mahoney for what she'd spent on the carnival. No—today, the last day of the celebration, would conclude with the first annual Mahoney Scholarship Award ceremony, where one student would receive a full scholarship to the college or university of their choice. The other candidates would get to split the money from the ticket sales.

Maybe the answer to all this was buried in there somewhere.

"Yesterday was crazy," Ned said, sipping my

Club Coffee drink before I could stop him. He recoiled. "Gross. That tastes horrible. Why would you drink cold coffee? It tastes like a caramel train wreck."

"Like I said, I've been here awhile."

"How did you get in, anyway?" he asked. "The school had to have been locked."

"When you've been solving cases for as long as I have, you acquire certain tricks of the trade."

"Such as?"

I lifted up my key chain and held it by one particular silver key, shaking it, and making it jangle.

"Where did you get a key to the school, Nancy?"

"It doesn't matter where I got the key, okay?" I said. "What matters is that I use it only when absolutely necessary."

I couldn't help but think that he was right on both counts, though—my coffee did taste like a caramel train wreck, and yesterday was crazy.

In fact, the last two days had been oddly interconnected with crime, each day with more sabotage and threatening blue notes than the one before. And those black smudges at the edges of the blue notes added a whole other layer of confusion.

It all started with Lexi Claremont, a client, who had hired me to infiltrate the it-girl clique, one of whom was my nemesis Deirdre Shannon, to figure out who had been writing a nasty blog about Lexi and sending her threatening messages. Thankfully, that mystery had been resolved well enough: Heather Harris, Lexi's supposed BFF, had been keeping the blog.

And yesterday the missing cash box money was the main event. First Ned, and then Mara Stanfield were accused, each tapped as the main suspect at different points in the day. It took awhile, but once I approached our town psychic (I know, I didn't think it would work either!), Lucia Gonsalvo, for assistance, she pointed me toward this video footage that not only proved Mara's innocence, but showed that the notes and the serious sabotage were the handiwork of this winking, masked mastermind I'd been analyzing this morning.

The once super-fun River Heights Celebration had been all but canceled this year because of the fires and theft and life-threatening parade sabotage. It had been a virtual nightmare, actually, but I was so much closer to finding the main culprit responsible for the bulk of the criminal activity. I couldn't help but wonder if or how Mara was involved. She had been targeted to be framed, which was no coincidence, in my opinion.

I rewound the tape again and watched the man

in slow motion. He snuck into the ticket booth, completely disguised with a mask, then left, but not before winking.

I paused the video.

"Did you see that?" I asked Ned.

"He winked," Mara said, standing in the doorway behind us.

Ned and I both jumped in our chairs.

"Mrs. Stanfield," Ned said. "Good morning. Nancy and I were just reviewing the video footage from yesterday."

"Find anything new?" she asked.

"Just this," I said, and rewound the tape to the man winking again. "Creepy stuff."

"I can't believe we have evidence of the culprit but can't figure out who's causing these horrible things to happen," she said. "You two should get out of here. I wouldn't want either of you to get in trouble being in here unsupervised. I think I saw George and Bess by the ring-toss game, Nancy. They were asking about you. Somehow I knew you would be here."

"I'm going to solve this mystery today," I said. "I promise."

"You need to be careful. This person is unpredictable," Mara said. Then she paused and looked at me with kind eyes. "Which reminds me. I wanted to thank you for everything yesterday. I don't know what I would have done if you hadn't proven my innocence."

I was shocked at her gratitude and hoped my surprise didn't show on my face. This woman never apologized, which only showed what a big deal her words were to me. "You're welcome, Mrs. Stanfield." I felt uncomfortable and changed the subject. "Lexi Claremont is presenting the Mahoney Scholarship Award tonight, right?" I asked.

"She is," Mara said. "Why? You think all the notes and missing money and fires have to do with the scholarship?"

"Everything from the carnival to the scholarship is paid for by Mrs. Mahoney and the Mahoney Foundation. Her husband was Cornelius Mahoney, a local businessman," I said.

"How do you know all of this?" Mara asked.

"Mrs. Mahoney has a very high opinion of me. She's one of my dad's clients, so I know her a little. And more importantly, I know how much this scholarship means to her and how much it would mean to whoever wins it."

"Okay, enough for now. Get out of here, you two," said Mara.

Ned and I stood and left the front office of the school, leaving Mara behind.

As we walked toward the front door I heard the machine rewind and the tape play back twice before we were outside. Mara stayed behind, watching the video footage just like I'd been doing since early that morning.

SQUARE ONE

"Let's stop by the fro-yo stand and grab a snack," Ned said, walking with me to meet Bess and George over by the ring toss. "I didn't have breakfast this morning, and I'm starving. I have to get something before I head over to the ticket booth."

"Absolutely not, Ned," I said. "My time there is finished. The only reason I worked there in the first place was to infiltrate that mean-girl clique and help Lexi out with her case. Now that her case is over, I have served my last fro-yo. You would have to either blindfold me or give me an amazing ultimatum to convince me to go back there. That

being said, if you need a fro-yo to stay awake at the ticket booth today, then by all means, go ahead without me."

Ned laughed and pulled me closer to him, hugging me again. "You really did look cute working the fro-yo stand, Nancy. I could have gotten used to having a girlfriend sliding me free fro-yos."

"You are the only person allowed to think that, but you also have to let it go, since it will never happen again. My fro-yo days are thankfully long gone."

"Do you want me to tell Lexi and Deirdre that you send your love and want to hang out later?" He laughed, enjoying the fact that he got me to smile at his teasing sense of humor. "Yes? No?"

"Ned, two things—one, it's too early to joke about my time at the fro-yo stand and two, do me a favor, be careful at the ticket booth today. I'm not saying anything like yesterday is going to happen today, but you can't fall asleep again. Mark Steele already hates you for doing it once. We got lucky that we were able to recoup the money. Just don't give him another reason to ask you to leave."

"I promise, Nancy. Will you make me a promise?"

"So long it doesn't have to do with a fro-yo," I said.

"Whatever else you do today, the first thing you need to do is get a fresh coffee." He took my cold

Club Coffee cup out of my hands and threw it away in a nearby trash can. "It's over. It's cold. It's gross. Get a new one."

Ned waved good-bye as he headed off for his fro-yo breakfast and I moved toward the ring toss to meet the girls.

It was odd to think about where this had all began.

I thought for the longest time that all the sabotage had been coming from within the clique. Like Lexi or Deirdre or even Aly Stanfield, Mara's daughter. But once everyone began receiving blue notes and one of the carnival food stations had a fire and a ride malfunctioned and the parade float had its tragic fire, it became clear that this was bigger than a high school spat. Whoever the saboteur was, he intended on sabotaging the entire carnival, not just a select few individuals.

Although it began with Lexi, who just so happened to be the face of this year's River Heights Celebration, it was a much larger issue than her.

Regardless, there would be no fro-yo in my future. Nor would there be heels or uncomfortable girly-girl clothes.

Today was an easy day of jeans and a simple yellow tank top—and most importantly, sandals *without* heels.

I met George and Bess both standing at the ring-toss

booth, where Sunshine Lawrence was enjoying her usual lack of customers and oversize cup of Club Coffee. Sunshine was sporting her everyday all black with heavy black cat-eye eyeliner. As usual, she wore her midnight black hair, short and cut at a dramatic angle, her blunt-cut bangs swept to the side in a single black barrette with a beautiful red heart at the clasp. She had a new stack of books behind the table, and her computer was open to a document.

Bess was decked out in a cute little sundress, typical for her, and George, like me, was comfortable in jeans. Both Bess and George had cups of Club Coffee too.

"Ladies," I said, "which one of those beautiful cups of coffee is for me?"

Bess and George laughed at the same time, before both extending their coffees to me.

"Both?" I asked.

"You texted us each the same order," Bess said.

"So we got two extra-large caramel macchiatos with extra caramel drizzled over the extra whipped cream with an extra shot of espresso," George said.

I couldn't believe it. It was like a dream come true—two coffees! But so as not to be a complete loser friend, I split the drinks equally among us, so we could all share in the delicious goodness.

"How's the ring-toss business, Sunshine? Are you

writing or reading today?" I asked as I approached the table.

"With all the excitement and activity of the past two days?" Sunshine said. "I'm writing a lot, actually. I've read eight books, too. So I guess you could say that ring toss is really slow, so I'm getting a lot of time to be creative."

"We were just filling Sunshine in on what we discovered last night," Bess said. "What we found out from the psychic."

"About the man in the video footage," George added. "How Mara didn't steal any money from the ticket booth."

"So you have to start the investigation all over again?" Sunshine asked. "That stinks!"

"It's the worst," George said. "The last two days have been nothing but hard word—and all for nothing, it seems."

"All the evidence we've collected is useless," Bess continued. "Or at least seems less helpful."

"Except for the videotape. We have footage of the person responsible," I said. "That's pretty important."

"But you still don't know who it is, which I bet is frustrating," Sunshine said.

"Girls, we have to remain positive here. Everyone is scared. Look at the carnival. Because of all of the sabotage, it's dead, empty. Everyone is scared to come because of the fires and notes and robbery. We have to pick up the investigation and find out who is causing all this."

George and Bess looked at each other. George threw a ring at a series of bottles and missed, the ring clanking around before hitting the ground. Bess took a ring from George and threw it at the bottles and missed, too. Finally I took the last ring from George, and without looking, tossed the ring at the bottles. The ring sailed through the air in a direct shot toward the bottles before looping around the neck of a bottle and sliding down.

George and Bess were stunned.

Sunshine laughed. "Nancy Drew, you are a natural at ring toss."

"We can't afford to be negative right now, girls," I said. "River Heights needs our help. Think of everything we've done these past few days. Think of all the people who've needed our help. We shut down that silly, hateful blog. We saved people from the float that caught on fire. Not to mention clearing people's names who were accused of stealing—Ned and Mara."

"We also solved the mystery of why people kept calling you Fancy Nancy," Bess said, stifling laughter. "That was a big mystery."

"Very funny," I said.

"Fancy Nancy," George said, laughing. "Heather Harris started a very good mystery by calling you that name. She really doesn't like you, Fancy Nancy."

Bess, George, and Sunshine laughed like this was something completely hilarious. I wasn't nearly as amused.

"And that was the only real mystery we solved yesterday," I said. "We never figured out who is causing all this sabotage, which is why we must do it today."

"More importantly is the *why*," Sunshine said. "The question of *who* is responsible is good too, but *why* they continue to do it is what keeps eluding us. The *why* is what everyone keeps talking about."

"Could it be a competing school who's doing this, Sunshine?" I asked.

"Maybe a rival who wants to see River Heights embarrassed or scared?" Bess asked.

"Is there a football rival? Or soccer? Or some other kind of sport?" George asked.

"I don't think so," Sunshine said. "Our rivalries are pretty innocent affairs. We're competitive but not violent, no nasty notes or arson."

"What about a grudge?" asked George. "Who would have a grudge against River Heights? Or the students? Or the Celebration?"

"That's a really big question," Sunshine said. "There are always unhappy people."

"Sunshine is right," I said. "Unfortunately, you know what this means."

"Yeah, we're back to square one," Bess said.

And we all hated to agree.

We were all quiet, staring at my ring, which still hung from the bottle behind the table. Sunshine handed us each another ring to toss, before stepping back.

"You all need a distraction while you brainstorm. This next ring toss is on the house," Sunshine said. "If one of you makes this toss, you can bet that the mystery will be solved by the end of the day."

George readied herself, aiming her ring and stretching it out toward the bottles, before pulling it back in slowly. Finally she spoke. "So, square one. After the fire at the sausage-and-peppers cart and the corn dog food poisoning, the food vendors were each targeted with threatening notes." George snapped her wrist and released the ring, which ricocheted off the side of a bottle. She was nowhere near close to looping the neck of the bottle.

Bess stepped up next. "The roller coaster was sabotaged to malfunction. Then the parade float burst into flames yesterday—right in the middle of the parade. Thankfully, no one was hurt, but the parade was the intended target. The notes warned us to stop the parade. We didn't stop it, and it was sabotaged." Bess bent her knees, before flicking her wrist and sailing the ring through the air. Sadly for her, she put so much force behind the ring that it flew over the bottles and slammed into the canvas wall on the back of the booth. "Oops," she said. "I was way off track."

"There is one other possibility," I said.

"Which is?" said George.

"The Mahoney Scholarship," I said. "The award ceremony is tonight."

"Really? You think? For a scholarship?" Bess asked.

"You mean that one of the candidates could want to win so bad that they're willing to put the other contestants' lives at risk?" George asked.

"The prize is a full college scholarship. That's an awful lot of money, especially in a time when college tuition is beyond expensive to pay for without loans," I said.

"Who are the candidates?" Bess asked.

Sunshine rattled off the names. "Shaz Morgan. Michael Kahlid, Seth Preston, and . . . Aly Stanfield. Two of them are girls, and you said that the mystery person you're looking for is a man, but maybe they know more about it than you think."

The girls were quiet.

"Aly seems unlikely—her entire room is a shrine

to Harvard, and her mother, Mara Stanfield, is the president of the PTA and the Daughters of River Heights. There is no way she would rig this so Aly could win—she knows if anyone found out, Aly's future would be affected. Besides, it makes a lot of sense that Mara would have been targeted yesterday. Maybe someone else is trying to remove her and Aly from the competition," I said. "Like a threat or black mail."

"Do you know anything about Shaz, Michael, or Seth?" George asked Sunshine.

"Besides the fact that they all embrace pocket protectors and a rigid schedule of homework on Saturday nights?" Sunshine snarked. "I know very little."

Bess tossed her a look. These candidates were smart and as deserving of the prize as Aly. It really could have been any one of them.

George finally snapped, "You need to tell us as much as you can about them."

"Okay, okay," Sunshine acquiesced. "Shaz is pretty much a tomboy, as you would expect a tomboy to be—not so into a girly appearance as you, Bess."

Bess smiled.

Sunshine continued, "She's into science and math and wants to go to Harvard Medical School. She and Aly have been competing for valedictorian since they were in diapers, but Shaz cares much less about fitting in. Aly runs with that whole mean-girl crowd, as you know. Whereas Shaz is just a total techie. That might be a good place to start."

Bess and I both looked to George, who raised her hands and said, "I'm on it, I'm on it. Shaz Morgan? Got it. Sounds like the spitting image of me, anyway. Send the tech girl to investigate the other tech girl."

I laughed. "George, never have you had a more appropriate subject to follow and research. Do you have any new gizmo or gadgets to use?"

"I constantly have tricks up my sleeve. Don't you worry about me."

"What about Michael and Seth?" Bess asked.

Sunshine giggled. "Seth likes to fancy himself a total ladies' man, even though he couldn't be further from that. He loves to talk about himself, look at himself, reference himself, and basically worship himself."

Seth Preston sounded right up Bess's alley as far as a smart, cute, charming boy was concerned. Although he didn't necessarily sound as charming as he believed himself to be.

Bess smoothed down her cute little dress and adjusted the straps of her gladiator sandals. "Seth Preston, you are about to be Bess Marvined," she said.

"You realize he could very well be behind all this

sabotage," I reminded her. "Don't let the fact that he might be charming and attractive distract you from seeking the truth."

"Nancy, I would never. I will remain professional. How is my hair?" she asked George, pulling out a compact and looking at her reflection in the tiny mirror.

"Which leaves us with Michael Kahlid?" I prompted.

"Good luck with him," said Sunshine. "He's the shyest kid I've ever met. And if you catch him on a bad day, then he'll be oddly standoffish. I mean, I keep a pretty low profile and even I barely know anything about him. If I had to point my finger at any one of them, I'd say he's probably the closest to being a true suspect."

As I listened to Sunshine tell us how little she knew about Michael, I noticed her blushing, a red patch spreading over her pale skin—the same shade of apple red as her lipstick. I leaned over, grabbed a blue receipt paper from Sunshine's cash box, and scrawled his name across it.

"Sunshine," I said, "is there anything you want to add about Michael?"

"No. Why?" she said.

"Nothing?" I asked.

"I hardly know him."

"But you wish you did?" I persisted.

She didn't answer, so I took a cue from our mystery man and winked at Sunshine. She continued to blush. I turned to Bess and George, who were ready to focus on their targets.

"Let me know if you find out anything interesting," I said, and then released my ring, which was another direct shot at the bottle I'd looped before. This time was just like the last—a direct hit, two for two, one on top of the other.

"Bull's-eye," Bess said.

"Oh my God," said George.

"This is a good sign," Sunshine said, sipping from her coffee cup, enjoying every bit of it. I imagined her coffee was not at all gross and cold like mine earlier today. I drank my new coffee, and it tasted like a delicious caramel treat.

It felt like a good sign, but I didn't want to jinx anything, so I said nothing and went looking for Michael Kahlid.

SEEKING MICHAEL KAHLID

I didn't have much to go on as far as looking for Michael Kahlid, so I thought the easiest thing to do would be to simply ask the volunteers that I passed and hope that one of them either knew what he looked like or knew where I could find him. This proved to be more difficult than I originally had thought, as no one knew of him or where he might be.

I walked across the carnival, checking out the food court and ride section also to make sure everything was running smoothly. I stopped at the funnel-cake stand and asked if they had received another blue note today, but they hadn't. I asked the people at the Ferris wheel if they had seen anything strange happening today, any strange behavior, stranger men, if they had had any mechanical failures, if they had received any blue notes. They hadn't. None of the above.

I passed the fro-yo stand, but only walked faster and said nothing. I didn't even look in their general direction. The last thing I wanted to do was engage with those girls again. I peeked over at the table as I passed, and the girls were sitting down, chatting and looking bored.

Granted it was early, but the number of people eating and riding the Ferris wheel and other rides was low. None of the rides had any lines waiting, and the benches surrounding the food section were all but empty.

In addition, I asked each of the volunteers, and not one person knew of a Michael Kahlid.

I walked to the ticket booth to check on Ned, and when I arrived, he smiled that amazing Ned Nickerson smile.

"Ned," I said, standing at the entrance, "I hope you haven't been napping again, because you remember what happened yesterday." I shot him a smile back.

Ned shook his head. "Yes. Sound asleep. All day." We both laughed. "Honestly, though, it has been really slow. I think the parade fire really scared people off."

"Did you enjoy your fro-yo this morning?"

"Can you believe that the booth wasn't even open first thing this morning? I mean, can you *believe* that? I just asked Mara, and she said it was because there were no real customers, so the girls decided to delay opening the stand. She also said that volunteers who wanted a fro-yo really didn't count. I am just beside myself over this." He smiled again.

"Yeah, I noticed the same thing walking around. The crowd is very thin compared to yesterday."

"Mr. Steele said that if things didn't pick up he was going to cancel the ceremony tonight for the Mahoney Scholarship Award too."

"Can he do that?" I asked.

"I guess so."

"Well, I'm looking for a kid named Michael Kahlid. Do you know of him?"

"Funny you should ask. He just stopped by. Said he needed to get into the school for something. I asked him his name, and that was the name he gave me."

"What did you tell him?"

"That it's closed to students. He didn't like that answer."

"What was his reaction?"

"He huffed at me and stormed off across the parking lot. My guess—"

"He tries to break into the school."

"Exactly," Ned said.

I used my secret school key to unlock the door again and stepped into the dark and quiet hallway. The floors looked super shiny, reflecting my shadow out in front of me.

I passed several classrooms, but no one was in any of them. The lights were off and the chairs flipped up on top of the desks. I had turned a corner and was facing another long hallway of darkness when I heard a squeak echo out from the end.

I moved quickly toward the sound, looking over my shoulder in case Mr. Steele or someone from school was following me.

Soon I saw a room with a light on. It was the upper school art classroom. It was all the way at the end of the hall, but if it turned out Michael Kahlid was there, it would be totally worth it.

A teenager stood inside the sunlit art classroom, molding and shaping a pile of gray clay—something that looked like a big bowl, but I didn't want to be presumptuous and commit to what it was and be completely wrong. That wouldn't be the best way to gain the confidence of a complete stranger, especially when I was investigating him as the mystery man.

29

I stood at the back of the classroom for a while, hoping he would look up and see me, but he never did. His focus and attention were solely on this clay bowl thing he was manipulating. Finally I cleared my throat, and he looked up but gave me only a glance. He hardly stopped at all.

"How did you get in here?" he finally asked.

"How did I?" The nerve of this kid, I thought. "How did you get in here?"

"I have means and purposes," he said.

"Well, you aren't supposed to be here. The school is closed to students without chaperones."

"Good thing you're here, then. You can be my chaperone, can't you?"

"You're missing the point," I said. "You broke into school. That's illegal. I am not your chaperone."

"If I broke into school, then I guess so did you," he said.

"I have keys," I said, jangling them at him.

"It's as simple as this—if you have keys, then you are my chaperone, right? Who else is given keys to a school? Otherwise, you're are trespassing too, in which case you and I are in the same boat."

This kid was getting on my nerves with his conversational tennis match. I wasn't about to let him score any more points.

"Are you Michael Kahlid?" I finally asked.

He cleared his throat, blushing just like Sunshine had done. "Who's asking?"

"My name is Nancy Drew."

He stopped molding and looked up again. "Seriously? Nancy Drew. *The* Nancy Drew? Everyone is talking about how you saved people from the fire yesterday and proved Mara Stanfield's innocence with the fake purse. Pradi versus Prada." He laughed. "Good work."

"I had help from some very important people. And most of those important people have been asking a lot of questions about this kid named Michael Kahlid, who is up for an amazing award tonight. Problem is that no one seems to know very much about you, which is why I'm here."

"Oh yeah. Like people care that much about a bunch of smart kids up for an award that ensures that they don't go into debt getting a college education. I highly doubt it."

He had a good point, one that ultimately gave him a terrific motive for sabotage. If he for some reason were able to scare off his competition, he stood to gain a virtually free college education.

"Why do you doubt it?" I asked, moving farther inside the room, sitting at the table across from him.

"I want to go to Cornell University, Nancy. Do you know anything about Cornell University?"

"No, I don't. Tell me."

"It's an Ivy League school. A very good one. A very expensive one. And for an only child, it's a school that two hard-working parents who don't have a lot of money cannot afford to send their only son to attend. So their only son spends his free time working on his art and filling out applications for every and all scholarships available. I can't rely on just one to come through. I have to play the field."

"Unless you get some financial help. From one of the scholarships."

"Exactly," he said. "You'll excuse me for not jumping for joy that you're the only person to understand that very real financial idea of college, but I'm working here. I need to focus my attention on something that really matters."

I didn't fully understand what he meant by that, so I pushed forward from a different angle.

"I see that you're an artist. What are you making?" Immediately after asking this question, I regretted it, because I knew his response before he even opened his mouth.

"What do you think it looks like?"

"A bowl?"

"See, you people, I mean, no one understands what an artist does. No one understands the artistic process."

"What do you mean? It isn't a bowl?"

"My art. You see it but don't understand it."

"Well, explain it to me. I don't understand why you're so upset."

"That's just my point. No one at this school even knows who I am. No one knows anything about me. You know more than most. I am smart. I am artistic. I am up for a scholarship, and you think I'm behind all this sabotage."

"I didn't say that."

"Well, you might as well have, otherwise, why would you be here? If I thought some kid was behind it all, I'd be here too. It's the next logical group of people to examine—the scholarship candidates. But I'm sorry to disappoint you. It's not me.

"No one knows anything about me," he went on. "No one ever has, and probably, no one ever will. That's the truth. That's just the reality of the situation."

"What does that mean?"

"I just mean no one cares about some quiet, shy, artistic kid who keeps to himself and might be a little blunt as a means to keep people away. I think this conversation is over."

"Michael, I don't think you have anything to do with the notes or fires or the sabotage yesterday. I just wanted to get to know you a little better. Since tonight's award ceremony is the biggest event since the parade yesterday, I'm trying to prepare for more sabotage to take place."

"Nancy," he said.

"Yes, Michael," I said.

"Don't lie to me. I have enough people in my life who lie to me. I don't need another. You do think I have something to do with all of this, don't you?"

"Look, I'll tell you the truth. Before I met you, I'd formed an opinion about you based on what I'd heard, but that's changed." Actually, I wasn't sure what I thought of him at this point, but I wanted him to believe what I said.

"Thanks for being honest." Michael stood up and pointed to the door. "I would like you to leave now. I have to finish this bowl and I would like to do so in private, please."

"If it's not a bowl, then would you tell me what it is? A plate? A vase? What?" I was sure these guesses were wrong as well, but I wanted to try one last time to get him to open up. But Michael was closed off and giving me no new information.

"Let's just call it a bowl and leave it at that."

THREE SUSPECTS

O n my way back across the parking lot from the school to the food court, I noticed the line to the ticket booth at the entrance to the carnival and was excited to see crowds of people arriving. How exciting! This was a great sign. The fear of the past two days had to be subsiding if the crowds were coming back out. At the same time, it was a good reminder that the saboteur really needed to be discovered—quickly.

I passed Joshua Andrews, the baker who was angry at Mark Steele yesterday for not renting him a booth for his bakery.

"Mr. Andrews," I said. "How are you today?"

"Much better than yesterday, Ms. Drew. I finally have a booth," he said with a smile. "They gave me what I wanted, and I can finally sell all my bread."

"Really?"

"Mark Steele finally broke down and gave me a booth after he got the cash back yesterday from the ticket booth. I think he reconsidered and realized how popular my booth would be."

"That's terrific news. You *were* pretty mad yesterday," I said. "I'm just glad to see you happy again."

Mr. Andrews laughed. "I know. But all is settled now." He continued on past the ticket booth and up into the food court. Before he disappeared in the crowd, he turned and waved to me again, smiling.

Although the day had started out slowly, it was picking up now and looked like it would be very busy after all. Ned was busy behind the ticket booth, greeting people and selling them tickets.

I met George and Bess back at our picnic table to share what information we'd been able to discover. Both girls seemed somewhat irritated, which only led me to believe that their subjects had been either less than accommodating or complete dead ends.

George had this look on her face that I had only ever seen before when one of her new gadgets had arrived broken and she had to return it to the sender.

She started to talk and I could tell right away that she was not happy about what she had learned.

"Shaz Morgan and I could not have clashed more," George began.

"What happened?" Bess asked, sipping a new, smaller Club Coffee.

"We had so much in common that I thought it would be so easy. Boy was I wrong. At first she seemed to be interested in a lot of the same stuff that I am, but I found out that was most certainly not the case."

"Well, what exactly happened?" I asked.

"What *is* she interested in?" Bess said.

"Shaz is only interested in technology for the advancement of medical research and practicality. That's it. No room for variety. That's all she talked about. I would tell you anything else about her if she'd offered it up to me. Whether she liked baseball or the Beatles or reality television, but she doesn't. Or at least she didn't *talk* about anything else. Only that one very specific, very particular, very *boring* thing."

Bess and I looked at each other in complete bewilderment. This girl sounded like a perfect candidate for the scholarship. I was sure she had a very high GPA and had the extracurricular activities to warrant being at this final level of the award ceremony, but my main question was this—does a person who is interested only in the advancement of medical research and practicality waste time planning and executing carnival sabotage, intense note writing, and arson? My hunch was probably not.

"What does that phrase even mean?" Bess asked. "The advancement of whatever it was that she said."

"She is a super-nerd," said George. "She is interested in math and science, and math and science only. She is set on winning this scholarship and is already going over her notes for her acceptance speech."

"What?" I asked. This was interesting.

"That's what she was doing when I found her. Presumptuous much, right?" George took a long breath and exhaled slowly. "She totally annoyed me, like, immediately annoyed me. She was preparing her thank-yous. Granted they were all for her professors or mentors in those specific fields, but she made it look like she was a shoo-in. There was no doubt in her mind that she was going to win."

"Did you find out anything useful?" I asked.

Bess continued. "Does she have any enemies? Did she say anything incriminating about anything other than science or math? Maybe she's made some people very unhappy while she's explored this scientific field."

We all already knew the answers to those questions.

"You know, it's funny that you ask that. There was one thing that definitely came to light through all her medical nerdiness."

"What is it?" I asked.

"Shaz and Aly have a rivalry that runs deeper than anyone knows. The only thing is that it has nothing to do with science."

"What then?" I asked.

"Their GPAs are only one-tenth of a point apart," George said.

"Who's in the lead?" Bess asked.

"Shaz," George said. "Interesting, right?"

"Did she say anything specifically about Aly?" I asked, both excited and terrified at the same time to be hearing this. Depending on the answer, our entire investigation could potentially shoot off in a completely different direction.

"Oh, you bet she had a lot to say," George said.

"They always do," said Bess, shaking her head.

"Shaz didn't have any problem coming up with bad things to say about Aly at all. Aly and her overprivileged lifestyle. The main theme of her dislike of Aly comes from the fact that, like most of the kids at this school, the Stanfields are rich enough to buy Aly's way into any Ivy League. Shaz believes that she should win based on her merit alone, but that Aly's financial influence will ultimately win out."

"Let me guess," I said. "Shaz had to claw her way to the top."

"Exactly her words," George said. "She had to claw her way to the top, and the rich kids have an unfair advantage."

"Already going over her acceptance speech?" Bess said.

"There's no competition for her," George said. "She doesn't see anyone who could possibly measure up to her accomplishments."

This was intriguing—the first of three suspects, Shaz Morgan.

I wondered to myself just how much, exactly, Shaz knew about the outcome of the Scholarship Award ceremony. And if she knew she'd already won, had she done something to make that happen? If so, what could it possibly have been? The blue notes? The brick through Aly and Mara's window? It didn't sound like she was exactly in love with her fellow classmates either. This certainly didn't convict her of any crime, but made it more difficult for me to discount her as a suspect. Would she even hesitate to hurt them to get what she wanted? It was conceivable that she had a hand in some of these sabotaged events, but that was still impossible to prove.

Her answers were certainly leading, but not

concrete enough to focus solely on her as the manipulator of events.

"Now, there are three judges of this award ceremony, correct?" Bess asked.

"Yes," said George.

"Do you think she's capable of blackmailing the judges?" I asked.

George shrugged. "Is it possible? Sure."

"Do you think she did blackmail them?" Bess asked.

"I don't know. It's well within the realm of possibility, I'll say that much. She is a live wire, that Shaz Morgan. I'll say this: Next time, Bess, you are speaking to her and I'll take the good-looking boy."

"You realize what we need to do?" I waited for the girls to answer, but they didn't. "We need to find out who the judges are. And stat," I said.

"How do we do that, though?" Bess asked. "Because I think they keep that information secret. For this very reason, actually. So that people can't bribe or sway the judges in any one direction."

"Shaz said the same thing to me," George said. "She claimed to have no idea who the judges were because it was a secret in order to keep a level field of opportunity, or something like that."

"What makes the most sense to me, I think, is that we approach Aly Stanfield about this, since her mother is the president of practically every organization in school."

"They don't have a nickname for Mara for nothing," Bess agreed.

"*Supamom,*" I said. "If I know Aly, she'll tell us what we want to know; we just need to ask the right questions."

"Well, how about you, Bess? How was your subject? What did you find out about Mr. Gorgeous Boy?" George asked, still holding a grudge that she'd had to investigate the dull and boring Shaz.

"As you both know, I was very excited to meet Seth Preston."

"You practically ran out of here," said George. "I'd say that you being excited is an extreme understatement."

"Give me a good-looking man any day of the week, right?" Bess closed her eyes and collected herself. "Was he handsome? Yes, Seth Preston was handsome. Was I excited for him to open his mouth and speak? Absolutely. When he eventually did speak, did he say anything of importance? Absolutely not."

"What *did* he say?" asked George.

"He was *waaaaay* too into himself and spent most of the time trying to convince me to escort him to the Award ceremony. The only problem was that he kept talking to me about himself in third person. So gross."

"He did realize that you weren't hitting on him?" I asked. "He must have known by the types of questions you were asking that you were digging for information? No one is that dumb."

"You would think so," Bess said. "But, sadly, no. He had no idea. When I asked him why he hadn't asked anyone as a date to the ceremony, he told me he already had a date but that I was way hotter and he'd dump his current date in a second if I agreed to go with him. He preferred to be seen with a *hottie*, not a *nottie*."

"Gross," I said.

"Double gross," George said.

"Well, what did you say?" I asked. "How does one handle that situation?"

"Nancy, are you kidding me? I said no. It was an easy situation to handle."

"We can agree that he is a slimeball," I said. "No argument here. But is he capable of committing any of the crimes we've seen these past few days? Do you think he's responsible for all the sabotage?"

Bess thought for a minute, then responded, "Anyone who speaks about himself in the third person is capable of anything. I wouldn't rule him out of anything. But honestly, I don't think so."

"How does someone talk in the third person?" George asked.

"Oh, you want an example?" asked Bess.

"Sure," George said.

Bess cleared her throat. "Seth Preston wants you to go home, put on a gown, and be his date for the ceremony tonight. Seth thinks you are way hotter than his current date. Seth Preston is happy to be Seth Preston because Seth Preston is one awesome dude. Seth wants to date you tonight."

"Really?" I asked.

"Truly," Bess said.

"I'm afraid we have three suspects," I said.

"Really?" asked Bess.

"Michael Kahlid is an artist with an edge. Like a lot of these candidates, he also wants to attend an Ivy League school and was very evasive when it came to answering my questions. He didn't say anything to rule him out as a suspect and avoided questions that made him sound more like a suspect."

"He's an artist?" George asked.

"He was sculpting clay when I found him, and he called himself and artist too. He struck me as intense and very sensitive."

"What was he making?" asked Bess.

"I thought he was making a bowl, but when I asked that very question and guessed it was a bowl, he freaked out. Clearly it wasn't a bowl, but I have no idea what it was meant to be."

"Suspect three?" Bess asked.

"We have three suspects that we need to narrow down to one." I grabbed George's arm and looked at her watch. "We have four hours. Four hours and counting until the awards ceremony."

"What do we do now?" said Bess.

"I suck it up and go get a fro-yo," I said reluctantly. "Find Aly at the stand and get answers."

"Why don't we all go?" George suggested.

"Strength in numbers," Bess said.

"No, girls," I said. "I have to go this one alone. We'll have a better shot at getting the information if I'm going by myself. It'll be okay. I just need to do my best to avoid Heather Harris."

"What if she's there?" asked Bess.

"Then I'll just have to deal as best I can."

"Prepare yourself to be called Fancy Nancy," Bess said.

"Yeah, oh jeez. I can't wait," I said.

5

THREE JUDGES

As I approached the fro-yo stand, the mean girls behind the table all shot me evil looks. I'd figured that would be their reaction, but I needed to speak with Aly, so I pushed forward. I wasn't surprised, and it didn't hurt my feelings at all. I was entering enemy territory with a mission and had to stick to the plan.

Yesterday we had all been friends, or at least tolerant of one another, but I'd also infiltrated their inner circle to find out who was writing that nasty blog. Now that the investigation was over, things were a little more difficult. I knew what I was up against and needed to keep my emotions in check.

I hated this moment more than anyone could possibly know. It wasn't too long ago that I had been on the other side of things, wearing *too cute* clothes, pretending to be part of the group, volunteering to make fro-yos and figuring out the inner workings of the mean-girl clique to solve the blog mystery. This kind of pressure was all part of the detective job title, part of the ups and downs, the pros and cons, the expected hurdles.

I would say this, though—based on how put-together and well styled these girls looked, I was definitely feeling way more comfortable than any of them in their kitten or wedge heels. Bess loved that she'd gotten to dress me up for this assignment to become one of the mean girls and work the fro-yo stand, but I was so happy be back to my normal casual self. Sheesh!

I stood in a small line of customers, waiting to face the wall of girls as they moved about filling cups and cones with vanilla and chocolate yogurt. They scooped sprinkles and fresh fruit onto the yogurt with attitude. I was nervous to approach them and prepared myself for a verbal battle.

I cringed, standing there, waiting in front of the fro-yo stand, like waiting to be sentenced by a judge. But I reminded myself that I really needed to speak with Aly and get to the bottom of this Mahoney award thing. It was imperative to find out about the judges, who they were and if it was possible that any of them could be involved with the sabotage. Sometimes an investigator or detective needed to put themselves in the line of fire in order to find answers.

"Well, look who it is," Heather Harris said, stepping to the table and cocking her hip, placing her hand slowly at her side. It was classic mean girl in all the expected ways.

"Hi," I said, locking eyes with Heather and not breaking away. I didn't expect to be welcomed with open arms, especially not by Heather, but I wasn't about to let her intimidate me.

"I don't think anyone here has anything to say to you," she said. "In fact, after everything you've done, I'm pretty surprised you're actually standing in front of us right now."

"Heather, hello. It's nice to see you again." I kept my cool and tried to stay focused on speaking to Aly. That was the most important thing.

"What kind of fro-yo would you like, Fancy Nancy?" Heather asked. "I know that Ned stopped by earlier."

"He said you were closed," I said.

"Yeah, well, we weren't closed," Heather said. "Sorry. Well, no. We're not sorry. We just saw him coming and decided not to serve him. Because we don't like you." She smirked. "So we don't like him, Fancy Nancy."

"Funny. Fancy Nancy. That was a good one. Remind me to thank you for that nickname. I had everyone from my dad to my friends calling me that yesterday. So thank you. That was really awesome. And how sweet that you wouldn't serve Ned because you don't like me. Seems awfully petty. Not to mention good for business."

"And I guess I have you to thank for just being a major pain in my life. A cute little nickname was the least I could do. So glad you liked it."

"We can go back and forth all day long, Heather."

"Yeah, Fancy Nancy, we *can*. And you know what? I'd win the verbal battle too."

I held up my hand to Heather. "Despite what your ego might be telling you, I am not here to speak to you."

She closed her mouth and took a step back, surprised. "Who could you possibly want to speak with here?"

"Contrary to your crazy thought process, I actually need to speak to Aly, not you." I turned to Aly directly, who was standing sheepishly off to the side and looked just as shocked as Heather without looking at any of the other girls. "Aly, can I talk to you for a sec?" I asked. Then I turned back to Heather. "I just need to speak to her. Five minutes. And for a change, this is something that doesn't have to do with you."

Heather turned, flipped her hair, and marched off.

Aly glanced at the other girls, but nodded to me anyway and stepped to the side, inviting me to walk with her.

"Thank you, Aly," I said. "I know this isn't easy. Your friends pretty much hate me right now, so I'll keep this short."

"What's up, Nancy?" Aly asked. "We need to make this quick. I have work to do and, yeah, I really can't spend that much time with you. Fro-yos to serve and change to make, you know?"

"Right, you have fro-yos to sling," I said. "I get it."

"And I really can't be seen speaking to you for very long. No offense," she said, smiling sympathetically, I thought. "It's just kind of like social paralysis."

"Wow, okay," I said. "I'll cut right to it. I was just wondering . . . your mom does a lot at the school. That's why they call her Supamom."

"I know. I hate that name."

"Well, she kind of is a supermom," I said. "And it's totally not a bad thing. I mean, that's why I went out of my way yesterday to help her out. Remember? She was accused of stealing the money? And I proved that she didn't do it."

I knew that this was a lame way to get on Aly's

good side, but I needed to find out about the judges, and guilting Aly into helping me might just get me exactly what I needed.

"Yes, you really saved her. Thanks for that. I mean it. I'm not sure what she would have done otherwise," Aly said.

"Well, I have a question for you then. Is there any chance she mentioned to you who is on the panel of judges for the Scholarship Award tonight? I really need to know."

Aly laughed, looking around like police would swarm and arrest her for answering my question. "It's hilarious that you are asking me this," she said. "Just hilarious. I can't believe you don't know who the judges are. I really can't believe it."

"I'm sorry," I said. "What is so hilarious about me asking you a question? I have no idea who the judges are. Why would I know? I'm not even nominated as a candidate."

"Mom has been keeping a pretty tight lid on who the judges of the award's ceremony will be because, well, since I'm a contestant, it's essentially a conflict of interest for her. It wouldn't be fair for me to know."

"I gathered that it might have been a conflict for her to be a judge for a scholarship her own daughter was nominated for," I said.

"But she slipped up last night when she was

complaining about how the judges were acting like children."

"Really?" I asked. "Who in particular is being a baby?"

Aly looked around for the invisible police again and then leaned in toward me.

"There will be three judges tonight," she said. "Not my mom, because, like you said, I'm a candidate and she would obviously be biased."

"Obviously," I said, rushing her to get to the point.

"She'll be overseeing the panel of judges instead."

"Okay. And the judges?" She really knew how to drag out the inevitable and make me twist and turn.

"Mrs. Mahoney is obviously one of them."

This was no real surprise, as it was her award to give away. Frankly, I would have been surprised if she wasn't one of the three judges.

"But last night Mom kept complaining that Mr. Steele was holding everything up, slowing the whole process down."

Mark Steele, the math teacher. I thought that was kind of weird. First he volunteered to chair the carnival, which couldn't have had more problems over the past three days, and now I found out he had agreed to be a judge on the scholarship award panel? Since when had he been such an interested party? He wasn't exactly involved in school, but all of a sudden he was involved *outside* of school? He was one of the few teachers who didn't even hold after-school study sessions near finals. It was like he couldn't wait to get out of school at the end of the day. So the fact that he was an official judge on a merit-based award panel was interesting. But it was so hard to believe that I asked her again.

"Mr. Steele?" I asked, confirming.

"Right? I thought that was weird too."

"And the third judge?" I couldn't wait to hear who the third judge was based on Mr. Steele's presence. Was it Joshua Andrews, the baker? Chief McGinnis? Mrs. Gruen?

"I don't know if I should tell you," she said.

"And the third judge is . . ." I pushed her some more.

"Nancy, this is weird."

"It will only be weird if you don't tell me the third judge."

"You mean you really don't know?" Aly asked, almost giggling.

"Seriously. I have no idea. Why do you keep asking me that?" I asked.

"I just thought you would have heard."

"Heard *what*?" I asked.

"Nancy, the third judge is your father . . . Carson Drew."

THE CARSON DREW JUDGE CONFIRMATION

I texted Bess and George to meet me at the ring toss as soon as possible.

I couldn't believe what I had just found out. Carson Drew, my father, was a judge? So many questions flooded my head. First and foremost, why hadn't Dad told me that he'd been asked to be a judge? There was no conflict concerning me. He wasn't even associated with the school in any direct way.

Besides the main point that he was the third judge, there were far too many weird and dangerous circumstances surrounding the River Heights Celebration that I had a bad feeling in my stomach about the whole thing. None of it felt right or legit to me.

But who asked Dad to get involved? Was it Mrs. Mahoney? Or Mark Steele? Or Mara Stanfield? Mrs. Mahoney seemed somewhat oblivious to how things like a carnival or scholarship were operated and run. I mean, that was why she had a lawyer to help her—my dad! Maybe that was how he got involved?

Mark Steele seemed to have himself well tied into a lot of these events, but I couldn't think of a reasonable excuse for why he would have asked my dad. Then again, maybe it was Mara Stanfield wanting to better Aly's chances somehow.

I couldn't wait to speak with the girls about this whole thing and get their feedback. I wandered back over to the ring toss, still pondering the news about my father. A few teenagers tossed rings at bottles poorly, and Sunshine held a book in one hand, occasionally collecting missed rings from the ground with the other. The teens finished up and moved away, just as I arrived.

"Any luck with the case?" Sunshine asked.

"Huge news," I said.

"That's terrific. What did you find out?" Sunshine finished the last of her coffee, tossing the empty container into the trash. When she finished, she bent below the table and pulled out a new Club Coffee container, still hot, and took a long sip.

"Do you just have an endless supply of coffee back there?" I asked.

"I make sure I keep enough on hand for the day," she said.

"I envy you," I said.

Just then Bess and George arrived, both also carrying cups of coffee from Club Coffee. They looked like they were eager to find out the news I had just obtained from Aly.

"Why is everyone drinking coffee except me?" I asked, unable to contain myself. "This is completely unfair and earns you each incredibly bad friend points."

The girls erupted into laughter.

Bess doubled over, slapping her knee.

George turned away, wiping tears of laughter from her eyes.

Sunshine held herself up by the booth structure of the ring toss.

Before I could start yelling at them, Bess slid a fourth cup of Club Coffee onto the table toward me.

"Is that mine?" I asked.

"Yours," Bess said, smiling.

"Is it . . ." I asked.

"That crazy caramel macchiato drink you love?"

said George. "Yes. I don't know why you like it so much, you'll probably be hyper for days after you drink it, but we got it for you nonetheless."

I grabbed it, smiling, and took a long sip, enjoying the terrific caramel loveliness of the sweetness and whipped cream on top. They were truly amazing friends to have picked this up for me in anticipation of my return.

"I told you she would freak out," Bess said to George and Sunshine.

"I didn't believe you," Sunshine said. "I've never seen anyone react like that to coffee before. And I guess I know what to give you, Nancy, if I never need a favor from you."

"She *loves* her coffee," George said. "We weren't exaggerating in the slightest. She's kind of *bananas* about it."

"So you all planned this?" I asked. "Well, it was pretty nice and mean at the same time, don't you think?"

"So what did you find out at the fro-yo stand?" Bess asked. "What did Aly have to say for herself?"

"I found out who the three judges are going to be tonight," I said. "The first one is not really a surprise—Mrs. Mahoney."

"Sure," George said.

"The next one is more surprising—Mark Steele," I said.

"Weird, but not an insane choice," said Bess.

"And the third?" Sunshine asked.

"This one totally threw me. I was completely taken off guard. Ready for it? My dad," I said.

All three girls were silent. They were as surprised as I'd been. Bess kept looking at me like I was going to say *Just kidding*, like she was waiting for me to tell her the punch line. George just kept nodding. I could tell that she was rolling the thought around in her head, trying to figure out the angles, as I had done not that long ago.

"Why is that a bad thing?" Sunshine asked.

"It's not bad that he's a judge," I said. "It's strange that he would be selected as a judge of a merit-based scholarship. Plus, he's Mrs. Mahoney's lawyer—I wonder if that might be a conflict of interest?"

"You need to call him and ask him how this happened," Bess said.

"You're absolutely right," I said, and pulled out my phone, dialing right away. My father's number rang too many times, before I left him three voice mails in as many minutes. On my last message I made a final plea.

"Dad. This is Nancy. I need to talk to you immediately. Please call me as soon as possible."

I clicked off my PDA in frustration.

"You going to be okay?" Sunshine asked.

I hadn't realized that she was standing in front of me now.

"Do people in your family keep secrets from each other?" I asked.

Sunshine laughed. "My whole family is very secretive. We don't tell each other anything."

I nodded in agreement. I could completely relate, which I never thought I would. It was my dad!

"So your father is a contest judge," Sunshine said. "Why is this such a big deal? What makes this such a bizarre situation for everyone?"

I thought for a moment. "Well, we've talked to all of the scholarship candidates, and while none of them has a clear motive, the only one we think we can rule out as a suspect is Aly. But whoever is responsible for the sabotage is still out there. And now that my father is directly situated in the line of fire, I suddenly have a lot more invested in it all. "

"*All* of them?" Sunshine asked. A blush crept across her face again. "They all have a motive? Shaz, Seth, *and* Michael? Really?"

Sunshine was acting very peculiar. I couldn't quite put my finger on what it was, but her attitude and tone of voice totally changed when she found out that I had not eliminated any of the candidates (except possibly Aly) from my list of potential saboteurs. It was like she was keeping something from me.

"Sunshine, is there something about one of the contestants that you know but aren't telling me? If so, you have to tell me."

"What? No. That's ridiculous." She looked away and was suddenly busy stacking some rings.

"I don't believe you. Why are you lying?" I asked.

"I am absolutely not lying." Sunshine continued to busy herself cleaning the ring-toss stand, setting her book down to do a better job with both hands.

Conveniently for Sunshine, my phone rang. It was Dad. Bess and George kept an eye on her as I talked to him.

"Excuse me," I said to Sunshine. "I have to take this." Then to Dad, I said, "Dad, where have you been? I've been trying to reach you."

"Nancy, what's wrong? Where are you? Are you okay?" he asked. His voice was drenched in concern and worry. I could tell that he genuinely had no idea what I was calling about.

As far as I could tell, being chosen as a judge on this scholarship panel didn't even register on his mind as an important item to discuss with his daughter.

Unbelievable!

"Why didn't you tell me that you're a judge for the Mahoney Scholarship Award?" The words blurted out without any kind of filter or warning. There was a silence on the other end. I could hear him breathing softly, taking his time to respond.

"What do you mean?" he asked.

"Dad? This is a big deal to me."

"Who told you?" he asked.

"Aly Stanfield mentioned it in passing," I said.

"Well, I can say that your lying abilities may be good where other people are involved, but I am your father and your father can tell that Aly didn't divulge this information in passing as you so casually stated. Care to try again? My bet is that you found out by doing some kind of interrogation."

"It wasn't an interrogation."

Carson sighed. "Nancy, I know one of your friends is up for the award, and the judges are supposed to remain anonymous. But to be honest, I'm glad you found out on your own. Saved me from having it be a huge surprise tonight."

I felt a tingle go up my spine. Something didn't make sense. "Dad, how fast can you get here?" I asked. "There's something I'd like to talk to you about before the ceremony."

"I'll be there shortly, actually. Is everything okay?"

"I think so. I just think I have an idea of who might be behind all the sabotage. I'm not sure, though."

"This is good news," he said.

"Yes, I just want to talk to you about it in person."

"Grand idea," he said.

"One question before you go," I said.

"I'm listening."

"Who asked you to be a judge on the panel?" I asked.

"Well, I was told I was replacing Mara Stanfield when she had to drop out because of the conflict with Aly being nominated."

"And who called you about the change?" I asked.

"Mark Steele called me. Why?" he asked.

"Get here as soon as you can," I said, and hung up.

Bess and George were taking turns tossing rings at the bottles, laughing, joking, and teasing each other while Sunshine ran interference and laughed along with them. I needed to speak to my dad first about my theory, before I told any of the girls about it. It didn't make sense to sound any alarms just yet.

Besides, Sunshine was still hiding something too, and those candidates for the scholarship weren't the most squeaky-clean either. It could have been any of them sabotaging everything these past two days.

People seemed to be losing perspective here. Someone was causing all these horrible things to happen. There was a very real reason, otherwise known as a motive, behind it all. And I suddenly had a very strong theory.

If I could just sort out my thoughts about that kid

Michael Kahlid, then it might all make more sense. I had this feeling that there was something he was keeping hidden. Maybe it was in that clay bowl he was making. I needed to check in on him before Dad got here. If he wasn't making a bowl, then what the heck was he making, and who was he making it for?

CASH BOX REVISITED

"Everything okay?" Sunshine asked eventually, watching me stand off to the side after my phone call with my dad.

Bess and George continued to play ring toss, completely oblivious that I was even off the phone or that Sunshine was no longer attending to their game.

"Totally fine," I said.

"What did your dad have to say about being a judge?" she asked.

"Not much. No big deal." I suddenly questioned Sunshine's interest in the scholarship. There was something she was keeping secret. "He'll be here soon, and I'll talk to him more in person once he arrives," I said.

"That's good then, right? He's still going to be a judge?"

"I don't know. I think so. Maybe not. We'll talk when he gets here." I was purposely being vague and trying to keep her confused until she dropped this line of questioning. "Sunshine, I have a question for you." I squared my shoulders.

"Sure. What's up?" she asked.

"What is your big secret?" I asked, stepping closer to her, moving into her space, providing a feeling of pursuit and pressure, which sometimes played a psychological game on people, pushing them to telling the truth. "I know you're keeping something from me, and it's time to tell me."

"Excuse me?" she asked, her face twisting into surprise. "What exactly are you asking me, Nancy?"

"I think you know something that you aren't telling me. I just don't know what it is yet. I don't know if it's about the sabotages or the scholarship applicants or what exactly. I just know that you're keeping something from me."

Sunshine moved back to Bess and George, collecting more rings for them to toss and bustling around so as to avoid answering my question. I would have pursued her for an answer, but just then I heard loud voices shouting from the ticket booth across the school grounds at the entrance to the carnival.

I looked at Sunshine, smiled apologetically, and then hurried away from the ring toss and over to Ned's station at the ticket booth. My only thought and great fear was that he had fallen asleep again and was getting yelled at by Mark Steele or Mara Stanfield.

I would be back at the ring toss soon enough to get to the bottom of Sunshine's blushing, a telltale sign that she had been lying to me.

At the ticket booth, a small group of angry adults and frustrated kids were gathered.

My handsome Ned Nickerson stood tall and strong between Mara Stanfield on his left and Mark Steele on his right. Everyone was talking at once. Their voices were loud, and each gestured wildly with their arms and hands. They shook their heads and stomped their feet at various times to indicate displeasure.

It wasn't until I got closer that I was finally able to hear what was being said and who was saying what.

"Stop," Mara said.

"Mara, you don't have the right to stop me," Mr. Steele said.

"Is everything okay?" I asked Ned.

Ned held the cash box in a white-knuckled grip.

Clearly he hadn't fallen asleep, nor had he lost the cash box, which was a great start to this scene.

"Oh, look. Another *student*," Mr. Steele said, glaring at me. "I really don't think this pertains to you, little girl. You should go off and find another mystery to solve and leave us alone."

"I heard yelling and thought I should come over, just to make sure that nothing out of the ordinary takes place." This man was really getting bent out of shape, and I had absolutely no idea why, although from his past behavior, I knew he had a short temper.

Mark Steele stood with his hands in his pockets now, biting his lip, clearly hoping I would leave.

"I meant it when I said I'm not going anywhere, so whatever you have to say to Ned or Mrs. Stanfield, you can say in front of me," I said.

"He was trying to take the cash box," Ned blurted out finally.

"Ned, dear boy, I am chairing this event." Mr. Steele spoke quietly at first. But his voice rose as he went on, "YESTERDAY, MONEY WAS TAKEN FROM THIS BOOTH." He closed his eyes and put his head down, collecting himself, then he took a deep breath. He began again, more calmly this time. "Yesterday, money was taken from this booth due to your incompetence, Mr. Nickerson."

"I didn't steal the money," Ned said. "All I did was fall asleep."

"You're right," said Mr. Steele. "You fell asleep, allowing someone to sneak in and steal the box out from under you. And so today, right now, what I wanted was to take the cash box with me. There have been a lot of people in and out today. More people are coming in for the carnival. The award ceremony is tonight. And I want to store the cash box in a safe place inside the school until the carnival is over."

Mara, who had been quiet for a bit, shook her head. "That idea was never discussed with me." Her arms were folded over her chest. "And so I think Ned here has the right idea to stop you."

"All I'm trying to do, Nancy, is stop him from taking the money," Ned said to me. "I don't want there to be any more misunderstandings. Besides, I need the cash box to make change for people buying tickets."

I threw an empathetic look Ned's way—I knew he still felt bad about falling asleep during the five minutes the cash box money had been stolen yesterday. That's a tough moment to come back from—falling asleep on the job and then having to prove to your supervisor that you are not only the best man for the job but that the one major mistake was actually a fluke.

"Mara, I want to ask you a very simple question, and I don't want you to take any offense," said Mr. Steele.

"I can't promise anything," she said.

Mr. Steele lost control of his volume again. "PLEASE EXPLAIN TO ME . . ." He regrouped and lowered his voice again. "Please explain to me, since when does the chairperson of this event have to answer to the president of the *Parent-Teacher Association*?" He could barely conceal the contempt in his tone.

"Since when is there no authority for you to answer to anyone *at all*?" Mara fired back. "Who is your supervisor? What checks and balances are in place for you?"

"Do you think I'm behind the notes and the theft?" he asked.

"I never said that," Mara said.

"Listen," he said. "I just want to know why you think I need to answer to someone. Or better yet, why you think I don't have to answer to anyone."

"Then who? Who said it's okay for you to take the money?" she asked.

"Mrs. Mahoney is my supervisor," he said.

"She is the sponsor, not your supervisor," Mara said. "You are unbelievable, little man, you know that?"

Mark Steele reached for the cash box one last time, just as Ned stepped back and returned to the ticket booth with it in hand, closing the door behind him. Mr. Steele stood toe-to-toe with Mara and had a mini stare-down contest, neither saying anything.

"Why don't you two walk your separate ways," I suggested.

"I am the head of the carnival committee and run things around here," Mr. Steele said to me. "I am not ordered around by a teenage girl. Nor will I be bullied by another adult, Mrs. Stanfield."

"Rules are rules, Mr. Steele," Mara stated firmly. "There is no need for you to take that cash box with you without official instructions. Sorry."

"I really hope this doesn't hurt Aly's chances tonight," Mr. Steele said, standing down a bit and taking a step back. "It would be a real shame if a mother's ridiculous actions got in the way of her daughter winning a full scholarship to the university of her choice."

"Oh, Mr. Steele, you wouldn't dare," she said. "You don't want to play games with me. Not with me, okay? Especially when it comes to my daughter."

Mr. Steele's face turned an incredible shade of red, a ripe beet red, and in a burst of anger and uncontrollable rage, he walked vigorously away and back toward the school building, empty-handed.

Mara Stanfield watched him retreat to the school

before stepping away as well, leaving the ticket booth empty again, except for Ned, who was inside hiding from the heated exchange.

I was about to walk away when all of a sudden I saw someone exit the school. My target—Michael Kahlid.

He snuck out of the school's side door, holding something under his arm, wrapped in a towel. He couldn't look more guilty or up to no good if he tried. Michael looked around and over his shoulder to see if anyone was following him. He must have walked right past Mark Steele, but knowing his state of mind, I imagined Mr. Steele didn't even realize there'd been a student in the school without a chaperone. Michael walked toward me, before suddenly making a mad dash for the parking lot and disappearing behind a sea of parked cars and minivans.

This odd behavior of both the head of the carnival committee and a scholarship candidate indicated a series of bizarre motives at play. It was great to see Ned stand up for what he believed in, especially when he didn't feel right about someone else being in control of the cash box. But Mark Steele and Michael Kahlid both had a lot of explaining to do and hopefully would lead me to answers without making the situation more difficult than the sabotage had already done.

MY MARK STEELE THEORY

Back at the picnic table in the food court, which had become sort of a meet-up spot throughout the day since it was equidistant from the parking lot and ring toss, Bess and George waited for me to return from the ticket booth. Both were eating hot dogs and sitting patiently.

Sunshine was still at her ring-toss booth, unable to get away, which allowed me a perfect opportunity to chat with the ladies about her and to see if they'd maybe picked up on anything. I still felt like there was something she was keeping hidden.

"Nancy," Bess said. "What happened with Ned? We heard the yelling."

"Did he fall asleep again?" asked George, laughing. "I certainly hope not, because that would just be embarrassing."

"We heard the arguing all the way over here," Bess said. "People are saying that Mara tried to have Mark Steele arrested. Is that true?"

"Not quite," I said. "She and Mr. Steele had it out, though, for sure. Practically a knock-down, drag-out fight. He wanted to take the cash box money and keep it locked away in a safe place, so it couldn't be stolen again. But Mara refused to let him take it away from Ned. They argued over who had more authority in the matter. Honestly, it seemed to me that Mr. Steele just gave up, rather than lose the fight."

"What did Ned do?" George asked.

"I bet he was so scared," Bess said. "Especially after having been accused of stealing the money yesterday and almost getting arrested."

"He stood his ground and didn't let Mr. Steele take it."

I looked to the parking lot and saw Dad whip his car around, trolling for an open spot. He would be here any moment.

"Listen girls, I have a quick question for you. Do you think Sunshine's hiding something?"

"What do you mean?" Bess asked.

"Like she has a secret?" George added.

"Yes. I think she knows more about the award candidates than she's letting on. Every time I bring up the fact they're all possible suspects, she becomes uneasy and blushes. Either of you notice anything strange?"

"I hadn't noticed anything out of the ordinary, but I will keep my eyes open," Bess said. "Blushing is usually a sign of a crush on someone. Maybe she has a thing for Seth Preston. They would make quite the pair."

"And one more thing," I said. "My dad will be here soon. I'm going to talk with him about something possibly big. I think I have an idea of who is causing the sabotage and just want to get his feedback first, before I send us all on a wild-goose chase."

"Really?" Bess said. "That's great! Who do you think it is?"

"I think that Mr. . . ." But I was cut off before I had the chance to tell Bess and George my thoughts. Dad had made it to the picnic table faster than I had anticipated.

"Mr. Carson Drew," George said, pointing behind me.

Dad walked up in his trademark necktie, khakis, and sports coat, having come straight from his law office. He arrived at the picnic table and sat down, smiling at us. "Bess. George. Nancy. How is everyone today?" he asked. "It has been quite the exciting past few days at the Celebration this year. Will be tough to top next year." He laughed at his own joke.

"Great, Mr. Drew," Bess said. "George and I have been playing a lot of ring toss today, which has been fun."

"Yeah, and I've been having a horrible time of it," George said. "I'm thinking of not buying any more fun tech gadgets for a while and maybe investing in a ring-toss game that I can set up in my backyard, so I can practice. Either that or hiring a ring-toss coach to train me, because this is just embarrassing."

"Nancy," Dad said, "are you staying out of trouble today? I hope you're at least keeping these girls out of trouble."

I didn't say anything right away, thinking of the best possible approach, the best possible lead-in to this conversation. After a bit, I decided to just come out and say exactly what I was thinking. "Dad," I said, "I would never ask you to do something so serious without good reason, but I need to talk to you about some important and quite possibly sensitive information that you have."

"About what? What do I possibly know that is sensitive information?"

"It's about one of the judges," I said.

"Nancy, you know there are only two other

judges—Mr. Steele and Mrs. Mahoney—and both are clients of mine. You know that I can't discuss anything about them or their cases. That breaches any and all attorney/client confidentiality. I took an oath, Nancy."

"Dad," I said. "I'm your daughter. You can break an oath for me."

Dad shifted uneasily on his side of the picnic bench, running his hand over his head and rubbing his eyes. He adjusted his necktie knot and cleared his throat, looking around. I hated that I made him feel uncomfortable with this conversation and wanted to do whatever I could to alleviate the stress and anxiety of it all.

"George and Bess, can I meet up with you all later?" I asked. "I need to speak with my dad in private for a bit."

"Sure thing, Nance," George said.

"Good to see you, Mr. Drew," said Bess.

"Okay," I said, turning back to Dad after George and Bess had left and giving him my undivided attention. "I have a theory about Mr. Steele. I don't want you to shut me down right away. I need you to hear me out, okay?"

"I'm always here to listen to you, Nancy. I love you."

"I love you too, Dad. And it's because I love you

that I'm sounding the warning alarms about Mr. Steele. Something isn't right there. My gut is telling me he is behind all this sabotage stuff. It makes me nervous that he asked you to be a judge. It makes me nervous that he was around when the money went missing yesterday. It makes me nervous that he just tried to take the money today. Something doesn't add up with him. Am I making sense? I hope so, because I think you're the only person who can help."

Dad sat there listening. He didn't laugh or look away or ignore what I was saying. Instead he just took it in like he was listening to a radio program. He finally nodded and leaned in close to me. His eyes were serious and intense, filled with concern and worry.

"I'm listening to what you have to say," he said.

"I know, Dad," I said.

"I'm trying to keep an open mind about things," he said.

"What do you think?" I said.

"Mark Steele is a client of mine."

"You told me Mr. Steele is a client of yours, so you can't really talk about him. I get that. And you can't talk about Mrs. Mahoney, either. I get that, too. But what about Cornelius Mahoney? Did you ever represent him? Can you talk about him at all?"

Dad looked at me knowingly. "Cornelius was not my client. So I can tell you about him. In fact, he was represented by Deirdre Shannon's father, so I suppose I can talk about him just fine."

"You can?" I was so excited.

"What do you want to know?"

I grinned. "So that means I can't ask you questions about Mrs. Mahoney, and I can't ask you questions about Mark Steele, but I can ask you about Cornelius Mahoney, right? Anything I want and you have to answer honestly?"

"My answers would largely be speculation and not fact, but technically, yes, you can ask me questions and I will answer them honestly, so long as they don't outwardly incriminate my clients."

"Was Cornelius Mahoney a criminal?" I asked, reveling in the bluntness of my question. "Doesn't matter in what way—meaning that he may or may not have had redeeming qualities as a human being. Straightforward question: Was he a good guy or a bad guy?"

"You just jump right in, don't you?" Dad asked. "You would make a great lawyer one day, Nancy."

"Well?" I asked him again. "Was he good or bad?"

"He was bad, Nancy. Why do you need to know that?"

"I just need to know," I said. "I want you to tell me everything you know about him. Every little last detail."

"Will this help your Mark Steele case somehow?" he asked.

"It should help to clarify things a bit. Whether it will further incriminate or exonerate Mr. Steele has yet to be seen," I said.

"You realize that Cornelius is dead, right? His widow, Mrs. Mahoney, runs everything in his name."

"I know, Dad. Please. Just indulge me. Mrs. Mahoney runs all of these events with his money too, right?"

"Let's regroup, Nancy. Yes, Cornelius Mahoney was a criminal. Turns out he was one of the most crooked businessmen of his time in River Heights. He was a real swindler and got people to invest all their money in fake or falsely represented real-estate schemes and promised them an early retirement— millions of dollars in profit, and so on. A real nice, stand-up guy, that Cornelius Mahoney."

"So he was a fraud? How did he steal from them?" I asked.

"Well, certain people bought into his lies—say, certain clients of *mine*—and these people were later blindsided when they went to withdraw their funds from the real estate scheme and it was all gone. All their money was just gone, because he had been living off it. In fact, I recall a number of local teachers, one in particular at River Heights High, who had even been planning on retiring early and funneled their savings into his cheating real-estate companies."

Dad winked at me in a way that reminded me of the man in the video footage. This, for some reason, suddenly reminded me of Mark Steele arguing with Ned over the cash box earlier, and how he wanted to take the money and hide it away in a safe place. Could this all have to do with Mr. Steele getting swindled out of retirement money?

"What happened to the investments that people made with Mr. Mahoney?" I asked. "I thought real estate was lucrative and that everyone was making a killing."

"Well, eventually the company owned by Mr. Mahoney was investigated for fraud, and it was discovered that every cent that anyone ever put into it was gone. Many of the people who lost everything had to go back to work after having retired."

"Was Cornelius convicted?" I asked.

"Nope. He died before he could stand trial, and the victims never saw a dime returned to them."

"Dad?" I asked.

"Nancy, please don't ask the question I know you're going to ask anyway."

"Please, Dad. Was that teacher you mentioned Mark Steele?" I asked.

"It seems like whoever is responsible for these fires and notes and ride malfunctions could be seeking some kind of closure or revenge. For a person who was swindled, wouldn't an extravagant town celebration funded by the crooked swindler himself through his wife be the perfect place to enact one's revenge?"

Dad placed his hands over my own. "You're a smart girl, Nancy Drew. And a brilliant detective. Which means that you know very well that this case isn't even a case without—"

"Evidence," I finished for him.

"Correct," he said. "Without evidence, you do not have a case."

RALLYING THE TROOPS

D ad left me at the picnic table after our talk, as he had to go back to his office before getting ready for the award ceremony that evening at seven o'clock.

Although somewhat unnerved by my Mark Steele theories and the sabotages taking place over the past several days, he was also open to the possibility that I was right. His only concern was that I have hard evidence before I made any false accusations. He was right, too. In order to proceed, I would need to bring the girls onboard, get them up to speed, and prepare for the ceremony.

Bess and George walked back over, this time eating blue cotton candy.

"How did your talk with your dad go?" Bess asked, sitting next to me on the picnic bench.

"Very well," I said. "I learned new information that has shed some much-needed light on our investigation."

Both girls were silent, staring at me, waiting for me to tell them everything.

"I believe that Mark Steele is behind everything," I said.

"Everything?" Bess asked.

"Yes, everything," I said. "Well, not the burn blog, obviously."

"Examples," Bess demanded.

"The fires, for starters," I said.

"What?" George said. "Really?"

"The notes, as a quick number two," I said.

"I just don't understand why," Bess said.

"Also, the roller coaster malfunction and the parade fire that broke out yesterday," I said.

"What did your dad have to say?" Bess asked.

"Well, Dad said that Mr. Steele is a client of his and that he couldn't directly talk about anything having to do with him," I said.

"That stinks," George said, slamming her fist into the table.

"So instead, I had him tell me all about Cornelius Mahoney, who just so happens to be a common criminal and extortionist."

George and Bess looked at each other, shocked.

"He died before reaching trial, but my theory is that Mark Steele invested a lot of money with Cornelius Mahoney and lost everything, which would explain his hatred of the school. Ruining the carnival and possibly the scholarship award winner is his attempt to get back at Mahoney—only at this point, of course, it's Mrs. Mahoney who'll suffer the bad press."

"Are we pretty sure Mark Steele has been behind the sabotage of this entire thing?" Bess asked. "The blue notes, the threats to Aly and Mara?"

"The rigged ride, the missing money, the fires and food poisoning?" George added.

"I think so," I said. "But there are two things that still don't make any sense."

"What?" Bess asked.

"First, I saw Michael Kahlid sneak out of the school with what I am assuming was his clay bowl or whatever wrapped in a towel. If we believe Mark Steele is the culprit, then what in the world was Michael doing in the school? What was he making? And second, why was Sunshine acting so weird whenever we talked about the four candidates for the scholarship?"

Bess bit her lip and examined her perfect manicured fingernails.

"I know that look," George said. "What's up, Bess?"

"What look?" she asked.

"That look. That one right there," said George. "We're cousins. I know you. What are you thinking about? What do you know?"

"I know that look too," I chimed in. "What do you know that we don't know? Spill it right now."

"Okay," Bess said. "I have a theory about Michael and Sunshine. But just like you trusted your dad, you have to trust me."

"I don't know if I can take any more long-shot assumptions that can't be proven," I said. "This Mark Steele thing is a lot as it is. What makes you believe that your theory is the right one?"

"Just listen and make up your mind for yourself," Bess said.

"Are there facts?" I asked.

"Is there hard evidence?" George asked.

"Is this a wild-goose chase?" I asked.

"No. I just need you both to listen to me very carefully," she said.

George and I moved closer to Bess and listened to her story as she spilled all her little secret details, and by the end we all agreed that she was probably correct. That what she'd told us was accurate and would work toward facilitating an end to all these conflicts.

MAHONEY SCHOLARSHIP AWARD CEREMONY

The Mahoney Scholarship Award ceremony was held at the school auditorium, and everyone was there.

The girls and I had had time to go home and change into less casual clothes before meeting up outside the auditorium shortly before seven o'clock that evening.

We waited for everyone to pass by and find their seats. Our plan was to come in behind the crowd and grab seats in the back or hang out by the exit door. We needed to be able to make a quick getaway. It seemed like the entire community had arrived for this presentation, at least more people than I'd expected. People brought bouquets of flowers for the applicants and food from the carnival. Some had salted pretzels. Some had cotton candy. Some had hot dogs and hamburgers.

As the flow of people dwindled, we snuck in at the back so no one would see us.

"All right, gang," I said. "Stay close and don't say anything to anyone. We don't want to strike up any unwanted conversations. We are only going to be here for a short time before we leave."

"Nancy," George asked, "what happens if someone sees us leave?"

"Come on," Bess said. "Where's your sense of danger? Who cares if anyone sees us? We're with Nancy. She can talk her way out of anything."

"No one will see us, George," I said. "Okay? And if they do, my dad will be watching us to make sure we can get away."

"He knows?" Bess asked.

"He knows we're on a mission to procure more evidence. He'll cover us if we're discovered."

Family members and friends, teachers and administrators all gathered for the formal selection and awarding of the college scholarship. The four candidates really drew quite the crowd. What became clear to me was that it was a big enough deal for someone to commit sabotage on a grand scale. A full ride to any college was serious. Anyone—students or teachers—could be held accountable.

The room was packed wall-to-wall, with every seat filled. This was a good thing. The last thing we needed was for three empty chairs to appear and someone to usher us over to them so we couldn't get away.

The stage had chairs for the judges and candidates, right next to the American flag and a podium with a microphone.

The fro-yo girls had arrived, Deirdre Shannon leading the way. They sat toward the front, supporting Aly Stanfield, or at least appearing to support her. Really, I thought they just wanted to brush shoulders with the local media, who were set up at the base of the stage, filming the ceremony and interviewing attendees. Deidre was front and center with perfect hair and makeup, ready for the cameras. I really hoped that Aly would win, as I knew she deserved the scholarship, but the competition was very steep.

Aly Stanfield and her mother Mara arrived too, walking up onto stage, finding seats behind Mark Steele, the speaker, who was about to open the ceremony. Cameras began to roll and lightbulbs flashed as the ceremony began.

Joshua Andrews and Mrs. Gruen sat toward the back of the auditorium, chatting about his banana walnut bread and her brownies. Dad sat with them and kept looking at me and nodding. He knew what we were about to do. He looked around at the people near us and would point to them or direct me to them with his eyes, if he thought I should know they were there.

A mother and three little kids strolled in late and caused a ruckus. The kids were laughing and stomping their feet, and one of them was crying because she wanted to go back to the Ferris wheel. The audience turned around almost in unison to see who it was that was making all that noise. The three of us obscured our faces and purposely didn't make eye contact with anyone. Finally the woman and her kids made their way down the auditorium to several open seats. We were safe for now.

George, Bess, and I stood along the back wall and watched as everyone turned their attention to Mark Steele onstage at the microphone. He cleared his throat and coughed into the microphone.

"Hello, everyone. Please be seated. Please be quiet. We need to begin. Hello." He banged the microphone with his palm. "Please. Hello. Settle down now. Settle down. We must begin." He looked tremendously annoyed and flustered in front of the microphone. I didn't know why he was speaking, really. I had actually expected Mara to be the master of ceremonies, not Mr. Steele, but he had control of the microphone, so the event began.

Everyone finally settled down and Mark Steele sighed, then took a sip of water, collecting himself, before finally beginning. He opened his mouth and stared out at the audience but didn't say anything for a while. It seemed so long, like maybe five minutes, although I'm sure it was much shorter than that. But he looked lost. Like he was searching for something to say, but nothing was coming out.

"What is he doing?" Bess whispered. "Why isn't he talking?"

"He's making me very nervous," George said. "Like he knows what we're about to do."

"I think he's angry. I think he's so angry about something that he doesn't know how to be kind and generous with this award."

He was still quiet. The room was quiet too. A piercing squawk of feedback reverberated and echoed through the speakers and around the auditorium. Several children cried from the noise.

"Shouldn't Mara or someone go up there and save him from this embarrassment?" Bess asked.

"Part of me thinks she might want him to experience this embarrassment," I said.

Then, finally, after an extremely uncomfortable amount of time, he started talking.

"We are here today to award the Mahoney Scholarship to one of these four finalists. Boy, was the competition stiff this year. All very deserving of the money. We have so many bright young children in the world and in this community that it was difficult for the three judges to make a decision. Mrs. Mahoney, Mr. Carson Drew, and I worked over time to figure out who should be awarded this most significant prize. This scholarship. Worth quite a bit of money. For me, it was tough because I have such a high standard by which I measure talent. For example, I read five newspapers a day." Mr. Steele raised his hands and showed his fingers. "You can tell by my fingers. They are always covered in ink!"

Whoa!

George and Bess both tapped my shoulders excitedly on either. We all looked up onstage as Mark leaned over the edge and showed the camera crews that were filming his grubby little fingers.

"This is what happens when you read a lot of newspapers. Your fingers get covered in ink, and it almost never comes off," he said.

I turned to both George and Bess.

"The notes," I said.

"I know," Bess said.

"We need to tell Chief McGinnis," said George.

"Not yet. Not quite yet. We need more evidence," I said. "We need to go to Mark Steele's office and look through his paperwork for one more thing. One more thing to make our case more convincing."

"But Nancy, the notes," George said, jumping up and down. "The ink on the notes and the ink on his fingers. It's a clue. A fact. A whatever you want to call it. He is the saboteur. I just know it."

"His fingers are covered in smeared ink, I know. Just like the notes," I said. "It was Mark Steele." I said. "Let's all meet in his classroom in ten minutes. But we have to leave one at a time so as not to draw unnecessary attention. Bess, you go first. Then you, George."

One by one we began to leave.

First it was Bess, sneaking out through the back without being detected.

Next was George. She tripped and fell as she passed a group of onlookers, but they were so riveted by Mr. Steele's dull and boring introduction that they didn't even notice her klutziness.

Mark Steele concluded his inane speech before turning the microphone over to Lexi Claremont, who stepped up to announce this year's winner of the Mahoney Scholarship.

All four applicants stood to listen with eager anticipation.

Shaz Morgan. Seth Preston. Aly Stanfield. And Michael Kahlid.

"Thank you all for coming to this very exciting and important scholarship award ceremony," she said, looking at the four candidates. "This is a most prestigious award for a student with a strong academic background and an ambitious goal to succeed. I am proud to announce that this year's River Heights winner of the Mahoney Scholarship is . . ." She paused, opening an envelope. She looked up at the crowd. "The suspense is killing me," she said, laughing. "And the winner is, Shaz Morgan."

I couldn't believe it. I couldn't believe that Aly hadn't won. Instead it was Shaz Morgan, who'd been so confident that she was going to get the scholarship.

The look on Aly's face was one of pure devastation.

Seth Preston just seemed oblivious, like he was eager to introduce Seth Preston as Seth Preston and continue his third-person tomfoolery.

And Michael Kahlid, well, he looked angry, and before I had a chance to turn and leave, I watched him storm off the stage, as if he was protesting the decision by leaving. He reappeared on the auditorium floor, and I noticed he was carrying something wrapped in a towel again. He was walking toward Sunshine, who

I noticed was sitting off to the side of the auditorium. I knew that was one mystery I needed to solve, but I didn't have time for at the moment.

As much as I wanted to stay and follow Michael to see where he was headed and what he was carrying—or even stay and listen to Shaz's speech—I had to leave and meet up with the girls at Mark Steele's classroom.

METAL CABINET EVIDENCE

left the auditorium and ran across the quad, passing the empty rides and barren food court.

Everything was quiet and empty. The entire community had left the carnival for the ceremony. No one was around at all. The parking lot was packed full of cars too, not one open space anywhere. Now was the time for some kind of crime to take place. The sun had set and the moon began to rise in the sky. Darkness made things spookier and scarier. I had to get to the school and find the evidence I needed to solve this case for good.

The girls waited for me outside the main entrance to the school.

As I approached, I knew right away that I was going to "accidentally" scare them, because the twilight covered the ground in darkness and heavy shadows. I moved through some bushes, stepping over fallen branches, before leaping onto the pavement leading up to the entrance of the school. Both girls screamed and pointed at me.

"Oh my," Bess screamed.

"It's the thief," George screamed, and grabbed onto Bess.

I laughed so hard that I couldn't control tears from streaming down my face. "You two are so silly."

"What took you so long?" Bess asked, angry and embarrassed. "You nearly gave me a heart attack, I was so scared."

"Well, I have some news that will make you less afraid," I said.

"What?" George said.

"Shaz won the scholarship," I said. "She beat out Aly, Seth, and Michael."

"I can't believe she was right," George said. "She knew she would win. How did she know she would win?"

"It doesn't mean anything," I said. "I think we were just dealing with three very arrogant kids who knew they were smart. Aly not included, of course."

"Well, whatever the case, hurry up, Nancy, and

open the door already," Bess said. "We've been standing outside here for so long. It's dark, and someone could come and find us here. I don't want to get in trouble."

"You are such a scaredy-cat," George said, laughing.

"I just don't want to get arrested," said Bess.

"No one is getting arrested," I said, as I tried to find the right key on my chain to unlock the door. I flipped my key ring around a few times before finding the right key, then slid it in . . . perfect! The door swung open with a loud creak and whine. We all three stood at the entranceway and stared down the long, dark hallway, filled with shadows and blue light.

"I don't want to do this anymore," Bess said. "This is a bad idea."

"I happen to agree with Bess on this one," said George. "Nancy, we should just go back to the ceremony and get some other way to find the evidence we need."

"You two can go back to the ceremony. Fine. But I have to do this. There's been too much drama and sabotage for me to just turn back now. So if you're going to leave, then go now. But if you're going to stay, I need to know that you're in this to help me and back me up. I can't hold your hand all the way through this. So, what is it going to be, you two—the ceremony or the school?"

Both girls looked at each other for an answer, for one of them to make the final decision. Finally, Bess spoke up.

"We'll follow you, Nancy."

"Let's go," George added.

All three of us entered the dark school and slammed the door shut behind us, the sound echoing through the empty hallway. As we stepped through the shadows, we listened carefully to every little sound.

A drip from a leaky bathroom faucet.

Banging pipes.

Our shoes clicking and squeaking down the linoleum.

"I don't think people ever hear these sounds during the daytime, do you? Or do you think I'm being neurotic?" George asked.

"Neurotic," Bess said.

As we passed an open classroom a loud *croak!* ripped out from inside the room as a classroom pet frog began calling out to the darkness, which made Bess and George jump and grab onto my arm.

"You are both neurotic and unbelievable," I said. "Stop being so silly. You're going to get us all caught and in trouble. Remember that I'm not even supposed to have keys to the school!"

"Sorry, Nance," George said.

"Yeah, sorry, Nancy," said Bess.

"It was a frog!" I said. "Don't be afraid of a frog!"

We moved farther down the school hallway until we reached Mr. Steele's classroom. We turned on the overhead lights, then spread out and began to search the classroom.

Bess took his desk and pulled open each drawer, moving pens and pencils and rulers and erasers to look for anything incriminating.

"What exactly are we looking for?" she asked, moving aside confiscated cell phones and books students must have been reading in his class (several copies of *Canterwood Crest*, for some reason; horses must be popular this year). He hated when students read books during his class, but the word on the street was that his class was so boring that you had to read a good book in order to stay awake, which was funny because there were so many books in his desk. Bess looked through all the drawers but didn't find anything incriminating at all.

George looked through the bookshelves along the wall under the windows, finding old tests and handouts and magazine articles. But then she found stacks of newspapers, which on closer examination turned out to be only the business section of the papers. There were local, state, and national newspapers, as well as international and financial ones. Each section had notes written on it, and words or phrases were highlighted.

Notes like "long-term retirement plan." Highlighted phrases like "real estate boom" and "real estate is a key investment" and "invest your money wisely" and "beware of real estate vultures and scams."

"Hey, Nancy," she said. "Is any of this useable as evidence?" she asked. "I'm not sure what exactly you need, but these are awfully peculiar."

"Close," I said. "But not quite close enough."

I focused my attention on a giant metal cabinet in the back that had a lock on the handle. I took out a bobby pin and handed it to George.

"I know you're handy when it comes to weird things like picking locks," I said. "So can you do us a favor and break into this?"

"Gladly," she said, excited to take a crack at the lock.

It took only a few seconds for the lock to snap open. The door swung wide and a large manila envelope fell out, tumbling to the floor. Its contents scattered at my feet. The girls and I knelt down and scooped together the papers, stuffing them back into the envelope.

But then I saw something—a brochure.

I held it up and examined it under the light.

"Retire Early into the Lap of Luxury . . ."

The brochure had pictures of white-sand beaches, beautiful infinity swimming pools, tennis/basketball/racquetball courts, a state-of-the-art gym, and living facilities that looked nothing less than palatial.

"This makes a lot of sense," I said. "Oh, my gosh. We're getting so close to finding exactly what we need."

"What does it mean?" George said.

"Looks like someone's having trouble letting go of the past," Bess said over my shoulder.

"All of those newspapers and the ink on his hands and this brochure—it all adds up to something, but not quite what I'm looking for," I said.

"What more do we need?" asked Bess.

"This is all circumstantial, as my dad would say. We need to find evidence that is undeniable," I said.

"Well, we've already broken into his cabinet. Why stop now? We must be close," George said.

The girls and I continued to dig through the metal cabinet, when we found a plastic bag that contained a black hoodie, a black ski mask, and bundles of blue notepaper with ink smeared at the edges. We froze and stood back from the bag. We had found the thief's clothing. And it all made sense. The thief was Mark Steele. He knew where the money would be. He knew where the cameras would be mounted and, more importantly, how to avoid them.

"Whoa," Bess said.

"I don't believe this," George said.

"Believe it, girls," I said, smiling, but scared. "This is the proof we've been looking for. We found it."

"It's the thief's mask and hoodie," Bess said. "What does this mean?"

"The thief is Mark Steele," I said. "He stole the money."

"And set the fires," George said.

"And wrote the notes!" Bess said, realizing the truth.

"This is a huge find. What do we do now, Nancy?" George asked.

"I think without a doubt we've found our guy," I said. "Now it's time to tell everyone what we have found."

SABOTEUR REVEALED

Bess, George, and I waited outside the auditorium for my dad to finish up with the ceremony, so we could talk to him about what we had just found out.

Crowds of people started pouring out. Everyone left talking about Shaz Morgan and the speech she gave about her pursuit and investment in the advancement of medical research and practicality. No one seemed to understand exactly what she'd been talking about, but it seemed that this scholarship was going to be put to good use, as she planned on plunging into this field after college and wanted to fully educate herself in the field in preparation.

I could only imagine what Seth Preston's speech, given totally in the third person, would have been like if he had won. Seth Preston would have been thankful for the opportunity to send Seth Preston to any college of his liking in order to give Seth Preston the best possible education, so that Seth Preston could get a terrific job.

That did leave Michael Kahlid as a wild card in the back of my mind. I still didn't know what he had been making in the art class. He had remained somewhat elusive all day, and after I spoke to Dad and figured out how to handle this Mark Steele situation, I would need to put this Michael mystery to bed as well.

Finally, after all the spectators had left, the organizers and main parties began to leave together, which was more than I could have asked for.

"Holy moly," Bess said. "Here comes everyone."

"Get ready, girls," I said. "We're going to finish this right now."

Aly Stanfield and her mother, Mara, were the first ones to exit the auditorium. My dad, Mrs. Gruen, and Mrs. Mahoney followed quickly behind. Mark Steele, Chief McGinnis, and Ned were the last to exit.

"Nancy," Dad said. "You missed the ceremony. Is everything okay?"

"Yes," I said. "I'm fine. We've figured out who's responsible for all the sabotage these past few days."

"Really?" Chief McGinnis said, moving closer to me, very interested in what he had overheard. "Please explain."

"This is ridiculous," Mark Steele said, cutting me off before I could talk. "Why are we still listening to this teenager talk about her wild theories when this clearly should be left up to the authorities? I am sick and tired of her harassing innocent people."

"Who said she had made any false accusations," Dad piped up. "Let's hear her out and see if it makes any sense. I think we all want to see an end to these dangerous acts of sabotage, so what's the harm in listening to her evidence?"

"I just feel it should be left to professionals, Carson, not a child," Mr. Steele said.

Chief McGinnis held his hands up, stopping Mr. Steele. "Slow down," Chief said. "Take it easy. She hasn't even said anything defamatory yet. She has a theory, and I'm willing to hear it out." He turned to me. "Nancy, let's hear it. What do you know? Tell me. I'm all ears."

I took a second to catch my breath. Everyone had their eyes on me. Ned was smiling, eager. Mrs. Mahoney was anxious, her hand on her heart. Chief had his arms crossed over his chest. Dad had his arm over my shoulders. Bess and George stood in the back of the group with their eyes on Mr. Steele. And he was firing nasty dagger eyes at me. It was all so stressful, I couldn't believe it. But I believed in what I was about to say.

"It was Mr. Steele," I blurted out. "He is behind everything. The notes. The fires. The robbery of the cash box. He has been terrorizing the Celebration. He is to blame for everything."

For a minute everyone just stared at me. No one said anything. I wasn't sure if it was because they didn't believe me or if it was too far-fetched or what exactly.

"Are you kidding me?" Mr. Steele finally said with an aggressive attitude. "Are you seriously entertaining this silly accusation? How could I possibly be behind all these shenanigans? Unbelievable. I don't need this. I have a carnival to oversee and finish up." He started to walk off, but Chief McGinnis grabbed him by the arm and pulled him back toward the group.

"Let's hear the girl out and not rush to judgment," Chief said.

"Right," said Dad. "My daughter isn't going to accuse anyone without evidence. So, Nancy, that is an interesting accusation, but what do you have to back it up?"

"While everyone was at the ceremony, Bess and

George and I went to his classroom to look for evidence."

"That's trespassing," Mr. Steele said.

"It's not," said Mara. "She's a volunteer. She's been working at the fro-yo stand. She is allowed to be on school grounds."

"Then it is illegal for her to have searched my classroom. Doesn't she need a warrant or something to be able to go through my personal belongings?" Mr. Steele asked.

"No," Chief said. "This is a school, not a private residence. A warrant is not needed. Anyone has the right to search and seizure." He looked at Mr. Steele. "Now, quiet." He looked back to me. "Please. Continue."

"We found some interesting things. First of all, we found stacks of newspapers from all over the country," I said.

"All over the world," George added.

"And remember when we examined all the notes that had been left for everyone the past few days? There were ink smudges all around the edges that we determined to be a special kind of ink used in newspaper print," said Bess.

"So we figured out that whoever wrote those notes was an avid newspaper reader," I said. "He even said it in his speech tonight. It was the last thing we heard before we left for his classroom, that he read all those newspapers every day and showed us his fingers. Look at his hands."

Chief McGinnis lifted Mr. Steele's hands and examined the pads of his fingers, each covered with black ink.

"This is ridiculous," Mr. Steele said. "Completely circumstantial. It doesn't prove anything except that I read."

"I have to agree with Mark," said Chief. "The ink smudges and newspapers, while certainly interesting and curious, do not prove that he's behind all the sabotage. I would need a lot more than that."

Bess pulled out the retirement brochure and handed it to Chief.

"We found this, too," she said. "In his locked closet."

Mr. Steele suddenly got more nervous and fidgety. He looked scared. "You broke into my cabinet? Now that must be some kind of crime. Breaking and entering or something."

"School property," replied the Chief.

"What does this mean?" Mrs. Mahoney asked, suddenly becoming interested. "How does this brochure factor in?"

"Mr. Steele had been saving his money to retire early, but he lost it all in a real-estate scam," I said.

"Lies," he said. "All sad and ridiculous lies."

"Nancy," said Dad. "We need more than this. Do you have anything else? These aren't enough for us to take seriously."

I pulled out a plastic bag.

"How about this?" I asked, and removed the ski mask, hooded sweatshirt, and blank blue notepapers with ink smudges on them. The ink smudges had full fingerprints along the edges.

"We'd be willing to bet that the fingerprints at the edges match Mr. Steele's fingerprints," Bess said.

"And that the hairs inside the ski mask would match his," George said.

"He had access. He had means. He had motive. He held on to the evidence," I said. "Mark Steele is the saboteur."

"Liar. These are lies, and Nancy Drew is a liar," Mr. Steele said.

"Where did you find the sweatshirt and mask?" Dad asked me.

"We broke into his locked metal cabinet and found them stuffed in the back. I'm sorry for being sneaky and having to go behind everyone's back, but I didn't want to make any accusations unless I knew for sure." I turned to Mrs. Mahoney. "I'm sorry, Mrs. Mahoney. I don't mean to dampen the festivities at all."

"Not at all, dearie," she said. "I'm glad someone

was able to finally find some answers. This is great news."

"It isn't great news," said Mr. Steele. "Nancy Drew was a student in my math class. And let's be honest, Nancy. You weren't the best student. In fact, if memory serves me correctly, you actually failed a few tests in my class. So it can be argued that you've had it in for me for a while now. Taking it a step further, your excuses to me about why you failed your tests were that you had been preoccupied with solving crimes. So between your prior excuses and failure at math, it can be deduced that your reasoning skills are not all that well developed."

"Watch yourself, Mark," said Dad. "That's my daughter you're talking about, so be careful about what exactly you're saying."

"Hold on. Hold on. Stop the presses a second. I don't understand something," Chief said. "This evidence, while certainly strong and incriminating, leaves me wondering about motive."

"The story is pretty simple, actually," Dad said, stepping forward. "Mark Steele gave Mrs. Mahoney's husband, Cornelius, all his savings to invest in a real-estate plan, and all his money disappeared. It was a scam. Cornelius stole it. And when Cornelius passed away, so did the possibility of ever recouping it. I know this because Mark is a client of mine, but now that I know he put children in danger by sabotaging the Celebration, I no longer want to represent him. You'll have to find another lawyer, Mark. And by the way, this means that I am no longer bound by attorney/client privilege."

"Mark Steele has been trying to get back at Mrs. Mahoney for what Cornelius did to him, and that is why he threatened everyone with notes and sabotaged the roller coaster and threw a brick through the Stanfields' window and stole the cash box. He was terrorizing everyone involved," I said. "Unfortunately, he was a victim years ago and couldn't retire because he lost everything to Cornelius's scam, so instead of fighting back in a legal manner, he fought back illegally and dangerously."

Chief McGinnis stepped closer to Mark Steele. "Is this correct? Did you lose everything to Cornelius?"

Mr. Steele was quiet for the first time in a while. He looked at his hands, picking at the ink-stained skin, as if trying to erase it.

"Mark?" Dad asked. "Are you listening to us?"

"Mr. Steele," I said, standing next to him now. "We know it was you. It explains why you've been acting so angry and accusing everyone around you. You wanted to cast as much doubt onto everyone else as possible. Onto Mara. Onto Ned."

"Did you set the fire on the float?" Mara asked.

"Tell me you didn't put all of those kids' lives in jeopardy. That would just be unforgivable, Mark. So many people could have been hurt or even killed."

Finally, without warning, Mark Steele broke. "YES! YES! YES!" He was pacing now. "It was me. But if it wasn't for Cornelius Mahoney. . . I swear. Cornelius Mahoney ruined me. He ruined my life. Stole all my money, and I had nothing left. I am astonished and completely disgusted that everyone in town is revering the Mahoneys as some kind of heroes after everything he did to drive people to financial ruin. I'm not the only one either. I am just the only one to do something about it. I wasn't about to take it sitting down." Mark Steele approached me. "And you. I can't believe you, you little girl. You just can't mind your own business. My entire life was ruined by her husband," he said, pointing at Mrs. Mahoney.

"Mark Steele," Chief McGinnis said. "You have the right to remain silent."

"What?" he said.

"You have the right to an attorney," Chief went on.

"No way. You are not seriously arresting me?" Mr. Steele said.

"If you can't afford one, one will be appointed to you by the court," said Chief.

"Are you kidding me with this?" Mr. Steele said.

"Anything you say can and will be used against

you in a court of law," Chief said, sounding satisfied to have found the guilty party at last. He turned Mr. Steele around and slapped bracelets onto his wrists. "Thanks, Nancy," Chief said, pushing Mr. Steele away from the group by the handcuffs. "The law will take it from here." Chief took the plastic bag of evidence from me and called in backup to scour the classroom for more.

"It's over," George said. "We did it!"

"Another mystery solved," Bess said.

"This was a tough one," I said. "And I couldn't have done it without you guys. Thanks for all your help."

Mrs. Mahoney stood off to the side, tearful and upset, sobbing into a handkerchief. My dad held her in his arms, consoling her, listening to her.

"This is a sad day for me," she said. "My husband was such a loving and kind man. The person everyone knew in public as a thief and a crook was not the man that I knew."

"Were you aware of his illegal activity?" Dad asked.

"Of course not, Carson," she said. "It wasn't until right before he died that all of his bad dealings and real-estate and financial scams came to light. I was so disgusted and embarrassed that I've spent my time and money since his death making amends. I sponsor scholarships and town events. I give to charity and help out wherever I can. I may have loved my husband, but that doesn't mean that I loved his actions."

"It's a sad situation for everyone," I said, "but Mr. Steele put students in real danger for his own selfish reasons, and that is unforgivable no matter what the catalyst."

SLEEPOVER DECOMPRESSION

Bess and George and I sat around a tray of Mrs. Gruen's brownies in my living room, picking at the gooey goodness. It was the weekend following the River Heights Celebration, and Mark Steele had been arrested for larceny, arson, and a whole bunch of other things that I didn't even know about. Apparently, he had been up to no good for quite some time now, and his recent crimes had finally caught up to him.

The three of us decided to spend Saturday night together at a sleepover, and at the last minute invited Sunshine over, as she had recently become a close friend. There was still something mysterious about her, though, that had me thinking that she was keeping a secret. I wasn't sure what it was, but the sleepover was also a ploy to get to the bottom of that as well. Once we got her here and satisfied with Mrs. Gruen's brownies, we wouldn't let her go until she spilled whatever it was she wasn't telling us.

"I can't help but be reminded of the sleepover I went to a last weekend at the Stanfields'," I said. "Those girls have such a strict code of mean girlness that I can only hope Aly can move away from all that when she goes to college."

"I heard she got into Harvard," George said.

"She did," Bess said. "That's what her mom told me the other day. That although she didn't get the Mahoney Scholarship, she did receive an acceptance letter into Harvard and will be attending there in the fall."

"That's so exciting," I said. "But let's just hope that no bricks get thrown through our windows during this sleepover."

"And that there are no notes taped to them," Bess said.

"Exactly," George said, licking more brownie off her fingers.

"You girls did a great job helping me out during this investigation and I really appreciate it," I said.

"I can't be everywhere at once, and you each went above and beyond the call of duty."

"Of course, Nancy," said George.

"This is what it means to be friends with you," Bess said. "Always risking getting in trouble."

"In search of the truth," George said.

"Finding the guilty party," Bess added.

"And exposing them," George said.

"Well, we all did a great job," I concluded. "Now, when Sunshine gets here, which should be any minute, we need to find out the truth about her. Bess, what you told us sounds possible, but we need to hear it from her directly."

Bess had told us her theory that Sunshine was, in fact, head-over-heels in love with a boy but wouldn't divulge who it was. We each had a theory about who it was. Bess and George seemed to think it was Ned, but I knew that it wasn't. I had my suspicions. What I needed was for Sunshine to come over to my house and sit down, so I could ask her questions about it directly without her scrambling to get away and avoiding them.

The doorbell rang, and it was Sunshine. She stood on my front patio with a giant purple mug in her hand.

"Come in, Sunshine," I said. "What in the world is that? Looks like the largest coffee mug in the history of the world."

"Thanks," she said, stepping inside. "I am glad you like this mug. You'll never guess who it's from."

"I bet I can guess," Bess said, laughing. "A boy."

"Yes, it is from a boy," said Sunshine.

"What boy?" George asked. "Can you tell us?"

"Well, I suppose I owe you an apology, Nancy," she said.

"Why is that?" I asked. I couldn't believe she was going to apologize to me. For what? For stealing Ned? Was she dating him now? Did Ned dump me without me even knowing it? I guess I did need to work less! "Please tell me why you're apologizing as quickly as possible! I can't stand the idea of another mystery so soon after the Celebration case."

"Remember how you would review your suspects in the scholarship ceremony, and you kept asking me about Michael Kahlid?" she asked.

"Yes," I said.

"And remember how I would always blush when you would talk about him, and I would get all weird and nervous?" she asked.

"Yes," I said.

"Well," she said, "I'm in love with him."

"Whaaaaat?" Bess said.

"I didn't see that one coming at all," George said.

"Well," said Bess. "I did tell Nancy and George I

was pretty sure you liked *someone*, but I never would have guessed it was Michael."

"And this mug?" Sunshine said. "He made it for me. He said he always saw me drinking coffee from to-go cups and wanted me to have a big, sturdy mug, so he made me this as a gift. Out of clay."

"In the art room," I said, the light dawning on me. So that was what he was making. A coffee mug. Not a bowl. And no wonder he was so sensitive about it. He was going to give it to a girl he really liked, and he was afraid that she wasn't going to like it and possibly not even know what it was. Oh, thank goodness! Another mystery solved.

"Sunshine," I said, "I am so happy for you. Congratulations on your new boyfriend. You are very lucky. I met him in the art classroom when he was making your coffee mug, and he was very intent and focused on making it perfect. Seems like you two are a perfect match for each other."

"When he didn't win the scholarship award, I went up to him after the ceremony to tell him that I thought he should have won and I was sorry he lost. I didn't even get a chance to say any of those things, because he was already telling me he'd made me something. The mug had to dry and be glazed and fired, so he actually just gave it to me this afternoon," Sunshine said. "But guess what else he told me after the ceremony? He said he's had a crush on me for years."

"And did you have a crush on him?" Bess asked.

"For years too." Sunshine nodded. "But I was just too shy to say or do anything about it."

"This explains all your blushing," I said. "You almost made yourself a suspect, Sunshine, with your odd, lovely behavior."

We all laughed and moved back into the kitchen for more of Mrs. Gruen's brownies. Sunshine filled her coffee mug—which in my opinion still kind of looked like a bowl, but I was definitely not going to say another word about it—with the hazelnut coffee I'd brewed shortly before she arrived.

The River Heights Celebration was over, and everyone was safe.

One giant mystery solved.

One girl getting to live out her college dream of going to Harvard.

And one fine romance.

It's all in a day's work in Nancyland. . . .

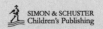